TIME UP

A NOVEL

JUSTIN McLACHLAN

BOXFIRE PRESS

ISBN 978-0-9827675-1-1

Library of Congress Control Number 2011913346

for Scott

ACKNOWLEDGEMENTS

I've got to thank Dr. Scott Sparks for answering endless medical questions, reading drafts and just putting up with me; Rebecca Gale for helping me reach new readers; Kris Goldsmith for all her work at Boxfire Press; Mom and Dad for sending money to buy a copy nine months before the book even went on sale; Morganna Conrad for fantastic editing and finally, my brother Craig, for his help and all his savvy advice — whether I asked for it or not.

The dead man didn't stay dead, and that wasn't even the worst part of the evening.

Trapped in a five-by-five treatment room, Van sat listening to a college-aged drug addict describe his back pain and need for exactly thirty tablets each of Vicodin and Ambien, please. He would, though, find twenty-five tablets of Percocet, which he helpfully explained was just oxycodone and acetaminophen, acceptable; at least he would if Van would prescribe the ten milligram pills instead of the fives and add on an IV drip of Benadryl before sending him home.

Van stifled back a yawn as the seconds ticked off in his head, beating like a metronome that he couldn't turn off. His patient hit on all the right words: chronic, severe, debilitating. These were the marks of a professional. He thought about the sandwich he'd left uneaten at the nurses' station fifty-eight minutes ago. He'd felt so behind earlier in the evening that he'd skipped the opportunity for lunch. His phone buzzed in his pocket, a reminder that he'd missed some calls a bit earlier when he was explaining priapism to a 52-year-old man who'd taken too much Viagra. The numbers had come up "unknown" so he figured if it were important, they'd call back.

Finally, the drug addict wrapped up his speech and looked at Van, expectantly.

"How did you say you hurt your back ag...?" For a second, only one, the clock in his head stopped ticking. It had been an incessant beat that had never, not once in his life, skipped and the disruption almost knocked him from his chair. He looked up at the clock hanging on the wall, across the room. It was clearly a minute behind.

"Are you okay?" the drug addict asked.

Van's pager went off, alerting him to a gunshot victim that had just rolled in. He excused himself and headed down the hallway toward the trauma bays that encircled the emergency department. He negotiated a path through all the people who'd crowded inside bay three so he could assess the situation. The victim was lean, trim and taller than average. They'd cut all his clothes off. His black hair, meticulously trimmed, was sweaty and matted with dirt. Van put him at around 45, 46 maybe. He was staunchly white, but looked healthy otherwise, save the gunshot wound to his stomach.

An anesthesiologist worked to put a tube down his throat and attach a respirator. One nurse did chest compressions and another, Jack, had been trying — and failing — to start IVs on his arms and neck. Van glanced over at the EKG monitor they'd

attached. Blood pressure was nil and there was next to no electrical activity in the heart. He told Jack to give up the IVs and prep
for an antecubital cutdown. Then he called for a crash cart and
slipped on two pairs of latex gloves and a paper gown.

Carefully, he peeled back the stack of trauma dressings the
EMTs had haphazardly taped to his abdomen. They were squishy
and soaked through with blood. He found a tiny hole underneath   ←
that didn't look as though it could *have* cause *d* all this fuss.

Van asked the nurses to help roll him, so he could get a look
at the guy's backside. There was no blood, no exit wound. Van
frowned as the possible problems that presented flooded his
head. Pierced intestine? Stomach? Ruptured spleen, probably.
If the inferior vena cava or abdominal aorta had been hit, there
wouldn't be much they could do.

"Do we know what happened?" Van asked.

"John Doe. They found him across the street, in the park,"
Jack said.

"Across the street here?"

Jack nodded. He passed Van a scalpel and some blue surgical
drapes, which Van laid out around a section of the guy's forearm.
Someone had already doused it with betadine, a yellow liquid
with an acrid smell that Van detested. Deftly, he sliced into the
man's arm, exposing a vein. He tied a ligature around the bottom
end, then cut the vein open and slid in a cannula. He tied off the
top to secure everything and then quickly sutured up the incision
while Jack attached an IV line.

Finally, an orderly rolled up with the defibrillator. Van
grabbed the two paddles and hit the big green "charge" button
on the front. After calling for everyone to stand back, he pushed

the paddles onto the guy's chest, sending a thousand volts of electricity through his torso, but the rhythm on the monitor didn't change. Van repeated the process of charging, pressing and shocking the guy over and over again, trying to jolt the heart back into beating normally. They paused only long enough to cut open his leg so they could start another line of fluids. But after about thirty minutes, the monitor flatlined and stayed that way. Van stepped back, tossed the paddles on the crash cart and dropped his arms to his side.

"Okay," he said. "Let's call this. Time of death, 12:32 a.m."

He pulled off his gloves and paper gown, tossed them in the garbage and then went straight for the sandwich he'd left at the nurse's station. But just as he took his seat and was about to start eating, he cell phone vibrated again. One of those "unknown" calls he'd received earlier had left a voicemail, and it was just now coming through. He listened, but it was just three seconds of silence. Telemarketers, surely. He slipped the phone back into his pocket, picked up the sandwich and was about to take a bite when Jack stepped up behind him.

"*Mein Fuhrer* is here," Jack whispered.

Dr. Greuenewald? Now? "It's after midnight," Van said.

He swiveled in his chair to see the short, bald German marching down the hall toward them. He was in a tuxedo. Not the sleek, sexy, James Bond kind, of course. His jacket was two sizes too small and he was wearing a cummerbund. It was, well, a cummerbund.

"Oh, hell," Van said.

Greuenewald came to a halt in front of the nurse's station and leveled a finger at Van. "My office. Now."

He didn't even offer Van a chair. Instead, he tore his jacket off in a fit, tossed it across the office and then thrust a stack of folded papers Van's way. Van wasn't sure of everything he was reading, but the words "Superior Court of California" emblazoned at the top of the first page were pretty clear.

"What is this?" Van asked.

"A lawsuit, naming me, you and half the hospital. The damn process server was waiting for me outside the Children's Museum fundraiser in the … the *kammerdiener*, Van! Do you know what it's like to be served in front of the mayor of San Diego? I do."

Greuenewald's always near-perfect English had given way to a thick German accent. Van took a second to digest what he'd said, translating "the" for all the "das." He was pretty sure there was something about a valet line in there, isn't that what *kammerdiener* meant? ⟵

"Van! Did you hear me?"

Mostly. "Yeah," he said. "A lawsuit over what?"

"Remmy Carter."

Greuenewald calmed enough to collect himself. He picked up his crumpled tuxedo coat and folded it over the back of his chair, then took a seat. Van racked his memory — Carter, Carter? He'd never been good at case management. Emergency room doctors either send their patients to specialists, home or to the morgue. There wasn't a whole lot of reason to remember their names.

"Sixteen-year-old, surfing accident? Eight months ago. Ring any alarms?"

He probably meant bells, Van figured. And yeah, Remmy Carter. He rung all kind of alarms. Van slunk down into one of two leather chairs Gruenewald had sitting in front of his desk.

"Everything I did was covered in the consent the parents—"

"Everything?"

"He'd broken his neck. He was on a ventilator, no brain activity, spinal cord crushed. He had no chance of recovery."

"So you just started experimenting?"

"No! Of course not. He was a good candidate for the treatment, my research—"

"A treatment you do not have IRB approval for, not to say anything of the FDA!"

"The parents understood the risks."

"Are you listening to yourself?"

"There was no way they could've known about the IRB."

"They know now. It is all there, in big, ugly, black letters."

"But that's— how?"

"You tell me."

Van looked through the papers. "Unapproved treatment" was count one, even above malpractice. There were a bunch of other things he didn't totally understand, but couldn't imagine they were good: negligence, intentional infliction of emotional distress, permanent injunction, compensatory and punitive damages. Remmy's parents were listed as the plaintiffs, along with his sister. The complaint was signed by a Mark A. Cooper, some lawyer who listed only a post office box for his address and no phone number.

"Where did the stem cells come from?" Gruenewald asked.

Van sighed. "I cloned them. From the boy's skin cells."

"Jesus Christ, Van!"

"We're not using any federal funds here, it's all—"

"You were creating embryos?"

"I was only trying to help. I was only trying to do what I thought was best—"

"Bullshit. You were trying to help yourself."

Okay, not completely untrue, in the broadest sense. But Gruenewald was missing the point. "I'm getting close to something here. But without human trials—"

"Did it work?"

Van shook his head. "Even the axons that survived the initial injury died. Slower than normal, but they still died."

Greuenewald rubbed his forehead, then leaned his chair back. "Have there been others?" he asked. Van didn't answer. He dropped his gaze to the floor and tried to think of some words, something he could say that wouldn't make him sound like Frankenstein. He didn't get the chance.

"Your medical privileges are suspended."

"You don't have the authority—"

Greuenewald slammed his hands on the desk, bouncing his keyboard and paperweights into the air. "Try and stop me!" he hissed.

Van fell silent. Greuenewald collected himself again, straightened his bow tie. "I'm calling an emergency IRB meeting tomorrow morning to discuss rescinding the research approvals you actually do have, Doctor. As for the medical board, well, I would suggest you find yourself a good attorney."

Van resisted the urge to defend himself. There was nothing he could say that would fix anything, at least for the moment, so he opted for silence. Greuenewald dismissed him without another word and Van left, tail firmly tucked. He returned to the emergency department, and two men in suits intercepted him at the main door. One of them flashed a badge.

"Dr. Jacobs?"

Van glanced over at his sandwich, sitting on the counter where he'd left it earlier. He was so hungry he felt shaky and light-headed. He'd not eaten since, what, 6:33 p.m.? And to make it all the worse, the place smelled like someone had brought in fresh, warm cinnamon rolls. He made a mental note to go looking for those, later.

"What can I do for you?" he asked.

They introduced themselves as detectives — Van had figured as much — from the San Diego Police Department homicide unit. Also not a news flash, considering the dead man still lying in his trauma bay down the hall. They asked, with straight faces, what had killed him.

"Well, I'm not a pathologist, but I'm guessing he died from the bullet hole in his stomach."

"That it?" asked the taller of the two, the one who'd flashed his badge.

Van shook his head. Aside from it not being his job, all he knew for sure was that the guy was dead *when* as he rolled into the emergency department and couldn't be resuscitated. He told them as much. "The nurses have probably bagged his clothes and whatever possessions he had."

"We'll need those," the shorter detective said.

Van went to the cabinet at the back of the nurses' station where they kept patients' personal property until it could be delivered to the hospital's security offices. He unlocked it and found a box full of brown paper bags, each stapled shut and labeled with the corresponding patient's name in thick black marker. There were quite a few. Aside from cutting off the clothing of most people who rolled through their doors, they also had to deal with things like shoes and cell phones and wallets that invariably came along. It took him a minute, but he found the bag he was looking for and passed it off to the tall detective.

"Just sign the custody forms and it's all yours."

The shorter signed his name on a clipboard the charge nurse kept at her station, and then they took the bag from Van. To his chagrin, they opened it right there on the counter and started rummaging inside. The taller detective glanced through the man's wallet, not that it would help. The hospital staff had already checked it for ID earlier. The shorter one scrolled through the lists on his cell phone. Van turned to his sandwich. He vaguely registered the two of them talking about the last few phone calls the man had made before he died. The shorter detective hit the call button and the phone redialed the last outgoing number.

Van was on his first bite when he felt his phone vibrate in his pocket. He dropped the sandwich in a huff and pulled it out. The caller ID said "unknown." He looked up at the detectives, then back to his phone, then back to the detectives.

"Shit," he said.

They questioned Van for more than a half-hour. He told them, again and again, that he neither shot the John Doe, nor knew who he was. No matter how many ways they asked the same questions, he said, his answers weren't going to change. Why the guy had called him — twice — or how he'd even gotten his cell phone number, he had no idea. Besides, he'd been in the ER all night. He couldn't have done it. The detectives eventually left him alone in his office, clearly not convinced of anything he'd said, and with a "friendly" offer to give them a call if he "happened to remember" anything "important" he wanted to talk with them about. The intimation wasn't lost.

Van sat, stewing, not sure what to do with himself. Now he had two reasons for a lawyer. If he didn't end up in prison, he was at best, out of a job — any job, if he lost his license along with his staff privileges. He shrugged. At least he'd have more time to surf. After a few minutes of restless leaning and spinning in his chair, he gave into his grumbling stomach and headed for the nurses' station in the emergency department. He got there only to find that someone had thrown the rest of his sandwich into the trash.

Jack was gone, and Sarah, his scheduled replacement, had already arrived. Van thought it odd Jack had left early, but didn't say anything.

"How's everything around here?" he asked.

"Fine. Dr. Parkins and Dr. Compton have picked up the slack, but things have really slowed down." She eyed him curiously. "You okay?"

"Yeah. It's nothing." Van paused, scratched his head a moment. "I think." He picked up a nearby patient chart and pretended to scan it. "Actually, I'm going to have another look at the John Doe."

He started toward the trauma bay, but Sarah called out to

him.

"What John Doe?"

"In trauma three?

She shook her head. "It's empty. Has been since I got here."

"That was fast."

She wrinkled her brow. "Fast? Jack said they'd left him lying in there taking up space for more than four hours."

"But I've only been—" he turned to look at the clock above the nurse's station. It was almost four in the morning. He looked back at Sarah, who was staring at him like he'd just broken into song.

"Dr. Jacobs, are you feeling okay?" she asked.

"Yeah. I just didn't realize how long we'd been up in my office."

She nodded, mumbled something about getting to work on the duty roster and left him, alone and bewildered. All he wanted to do was go home, eat, lie in his bed, sleep, eat again and maybe go surfing somewhere in between. He was completely lost in thought when he turned to see Dr. Compton standing in front of him, in the middle of explaining something.

"Dr. Jacobs? Did you hear me?"

"Huh? Surfing."

"What?"

"I was thinking about surfing. Where did you come from?"

From what Van had seen of him changing into scrubs in the locker room, Dr. Compton was the medical world's equivalent of a Details cover model. He was a good two inches taller than Van, had chestnut hair, emerald-green eyes, a chiseled jaw bone and a tan that would make even San Diego's lifeguards jealous.

"I was telling you about the guy in room 4. Cops brought him in off the street, the psychotic break guy? The officers have been waiting for a while, so I went ahead and looked over everything and then signed the orders."

"Yeah, thanks. Uh, he's violent. The officers will stay until he's transferred?"

"I won't let them leave."

Dr. Compton started to say something else, but Van was overcome with a wave of nausea that twisted his stomach into knots. He almost vomited. The next thing he knew, Compton was a hundred feet down the hall and moving away. Had he blacked out? Van felt his forehead. His skin was clammy and hot. He sat on a bench along the wall and waited for whatever the hell was wrong to pass. The night was not going according to any sense of a plan.

Why had the dead guy called him? Who'd shot him and probably even more important, why? Usually, when you shoot someone, you've got a good reason, or at least some reason. Van couldn't imagine what any of it had to do with him, but there were those unknown calls, evidence that he was wrapped up in something that he didn't even know about. And where the hell were those cinnamon rolls? The smell was irresistible.

He pulled his phone from his pocket and scrolled through the list of recent calls. He stared at the phone, thinking, for just a moment, about tossing it across the room. Wouldn't solve anything, but it might make him feel better. Probably not. He put it back in his pocket, and then continued on his way to visit the John Doe who'd died in his ER.

The morgue was on a basement floor deep in the recesses of the hospital. Van had never had reason to go down there before, so he wasn't sure what to expect. When the elevator door opened, he found himself in a small room staring at a man behind one of those security windows with fine mesh running through the glass. The attendant didn't look up as Van entered, but sat glued to a television screen, laughing raucously at an *I Love Lucy* rerun. He let Van pass without even checking his identification.

Van stepped through three different doors before he found himself at the front end of a long hallway, lit only by a few spastically flickering fluorescent lights. He squinted and made out a sign at the far end, above a set of swinging double doors that said "Cold Storage." He walked slowly, staying near the wall for guidance until his eyes adjusted to the dark. Once inside the storage room, he groped around until he found a light switch. A couple rows of fluorescents snapped on, casting a pallid green glow across the room. They flickered just like the ones in the hallway.

The room was a big, empty rectangle. The floor and walls were covered in the same dingy, ceramic tile that had infected most of the other non-public areas of the hospital. Some designer's idea of utilitarian chic, sixties style. The far wall was arrayed with twenty or so stainless-steel refrigerator doors, situated in two groups. It took him a few moments, but Van found the door marked with the chart number of the John Doe.

Cold air blasted him as he unlatched the door. He pulled the tray table out and unzipped the body bag a few inches, just enough to reveal the guy's face. Van's shoulders slumped. He'd thought maybe, if he got another look, he'd recognize him, but no. He could be any one of a thousand middle-aged, white guys.

Other than the bullet hole in his stomach and a faint scar above his eyebrow, Van didn't see anything real ̸ly distinctive.

"Good looking guy, yeah?"

Van jumped a good foot in the air. He turned to see a tall guy with neat, black hair and a shiny designer coat standing behind him in the doorway. Then he saw the gun: a .44 caliber Glock, nestled in his hand as casually as if it were a cell phone. Van rolled his eyes and muttered a swear word. He wanted none of this, but he was getting it anyway. He lunged for the gun, but the guy countered to the side and Van crashed nearly head first into the wall.

"What are you doing?" the guy asked.

Van reared and kicked him in the back of the leg, knocking him on his ass. The gun hit the ground and skidded across the floor.

"Would you knock it off!"

Van faltered for a second. That wasn't the reaction he'd expected. "Would I—?"

Before he could finish, the guy swung his legs and kicked Van's feet out from underneath him. He cracked his head against the wall and slid, dazed, to the floor. He lay there, crumpled like an old dish towel, as the guy pushed to his feet and then stalked across the room to retrieve his weapon.

Van ached and his stomach was rolling, but it was now or never. With every last bit of his strength, with every muscle in his body screaming, he launched himself onto his feet and across the room. He tackled the man and they both went to the floor in a heap. Van managed to claw his way to the gun first, which had come to rest just under an empty gurney in the corner. He hoisted himself to his feet and aimed.

"Wait!" the guy shouted.

"Not exactly in a waiting mood," Van said. His hands shook as the adrenaline surge faded. All the aches and pains of being in a knock-down fight reared.

"I'm on your side," the man said, panting.

"You're on my what? You just tried to shoot me!"

He shook his head. "I wasn't trying to shoot you. You jumped me when I came in the room."

"You… well…" Okay, he had a point about that. Whatever. "You always come in rooms guns blazing? Who the hell are you?"

"My name is Cal." He held his arms out in front of him, eyes locked on the gun. "Let's not do anything stupid."

"Too late."

"Look at me, Van."

"I am looking at you."

"Van, look at me. Look at me."

Van lowered the gun — just a little — and took a step back. He scanned Cal up, then down. Nothing really stood out. He was tallish, about as tall as Van. Short black hair, looked over forty. Van looked back at the John Doe's dead body sticking out from the freezer. Then he looked back at Cal. Then back at the dead body. Then back at Cal. Above Cal's his eye brow, just about two inches long, were the faint outlines of a scar.

Then, everything went black.

Van opened his eyes to the bright, stinging glow of the fluorescent lights in the morgue. He was on the floor. Everything hurt. Cal stood over him, asking if he was all right. Where'd the gun go? He pushed himself up slowly, glancing around the room.

"Seriously, are you okay?"

"I'm okay," Van said. "I just skipped dinner."

"That's not why you passed out," Cal said.

"What?" Where was that damned gun? He twisted his neck to scan the room, but he didn't see it.

"I took the gun back, Van."

Obviously. God, he felt slow. He looked up at Cal, aware for the first time since passing out that he was talking to the man who'd been rolled DOA into the emergency room some — however many, he'd completely lost track — hours ago.

"Why aren't you dead? Why aren't I dead?"

"I told you, I'm not here to kill you." Van relaxed at that, but just a bit. His strength started to return, enough that he thought he could venture trying to stand. Cal helped him to his feet. "But, someone else might be," he said.

Cal crossed the room and unzipped the bag around his still dead body.

"What? Who? Why?"

"I'll explain everything. Just give me a minute." He pulled a small leather case from inside his jacket pocket, which he unzipped and placed on the table. He pulled out a pair of tweezers, and then dug into the bullet hole in his — or, rather, in the corpse's — stomach. After a few seconds of trying, he pulled out the bullet.

"What are you doing with that?"

"I'm hoping this will help to tell us who shot me."

"I don't understand."

"That's normal. Is there some place we can talk, some place private? You need to change anyway."

"Why would I go anywhere with you? A few minutes ago you were just a dead guy in a freezer. You are still a dead guy in a freezer."

"You want answers?"

"I can live without them."

"Sure about that?"

"That a threat?"

"You know what? Fine. Stay here and fend for yourself. With luck, maybe you won't be the next dead guy in a freezer."

Cal turned and walked through the double-doors, leaving Van to stew. He crossed his arms and clenched his jaw. Hell if he was going to follow a dead guy with a gun around the hospital, taking orders and… whatever.

"Hey, wait!" Van called, chasing after him.

They took the elevator back to the ground floor, and as the doors opened, Cal poked his head out and looked up and down the hallway, like he was afraid of what might jump out at them. Apparently satisfied it was safe, Cal stepped into the hallway and motioned for Van to follow. They headed to the stairs, and Cal asked Van to lead the way to his office. When they arrived, Cal opened the door, looked around inside like he had when they got off the elevator, then indicated it was okay for Van to come in. He shut the door behind him.

"Change into street clothes."

Cal kept one eye on Van and one on the door to his office,

gun at the ready. Van had the strong sense that trusting Cal was a mistake. He also had the strong sense that arguing wouldn't get him very far. He pulled off his scrub top and reached for the spare T-shirt he kept on a door hook in his closet. He changed out of his scrub pants and into a pair of jeans.

"I'm assuming you know how to use this?" Cal asked. He handed Van a small, black handgun—another Glock. Van took the pistol and checked the clip. He nodded. Cal gave him a long look. "How's playing doctor going for you?"

"I'm sorry?"

Cal smiled and then winked at Van. "We can talk about that later."

"I think we'll talk about it now." He raked the chamber and pointed the gun at Cal.

"Well, I'm officially a moron."

Van stood, gun aimed.

Cal sighed. "We gonna do this now?"

Van nodded.

"You took a year and a half off between finishing your second residency, this one in emergency medicine here, at UC San Diego and coming back to work. You lived in Washington, D.C."

"I liked the city."

"No one likes that city."

"First time for everything."

"Unusual career path, though, wasn't it? You know. Not working."

"I needed a break."

"In the morgue, you took me down with one, well-placed kick."

"I got lucky."

"You're trained." He took a small step in Van's direction.

"I take some classes over in La Mesa. Krav Maga. I have a dozen classmates who could do the same thing."

"You're lying."

"Where are you getting all this?"

"My sources are solid."

He took another step, and this time Van felt compelled to back up, flat against his desk. "I think you're the one who's not telling the truth here, Cal," Van said. "I think you just walked off the mental ward."

"You took the Beltway from your house in Georgetown every day to Ft. Meade, Maryland. Drove a Volvo."

"I've never been to Ft. Meade."

"You speak Russian, Spanish, Farsi. Your German is a bit rusty."

"You've got me seriously confused with someone else."

"I get it. Admit nothing, deny everything, make counter accusations. The training shows like a road flare if you know what to look for." He took another step, closing the distance between them to an uncomfortable few inches. "So what does your training tell you to do now?"

Before Van could answer, Cal swung his free arm up and grabbed Van's gun. He spun his body around and pulled Van's arm under his own, immobilizing it. Van countered by pulling back on Cal's free arm, spinning him back around. Before either knew it, they were standing two inches apart, arms locked and each other's guns pointed at the other's head.

Cal laughed. "Very nice," he said. "Very, very nice."

Van shoved him off. They stood, a few feet apart, panting and staring each other down, both guns still raised.

"Maybe we've gotten off to a bad start," Cal said.

"Get out of my—"

Before he could finish, outside, the dull orange of the streetlights gave way to blinding, midday sunlight. Van spun to face the window, then back to look at the clock on the wall. It was barely after four in the morning. He looked at Cal.

"Why is it daytime outside?"

"You're in the middle of a pretty unusual event."

"No shit."

"Time has shattered. That's what's happening here, now."

"Time has… shattered. Time has shattered?"

"It's a lot to take in. But you of all people—"

"What is that supposed to mean?"

"How long have we been in this room?"

"Five minutes, nine… seconds." Cal lowered his gun, waiting. Van did the same. "So I've got a good internal clock."

"A computer has a good internal clock."

"Why are you here? What do you want?"

"We think you can fix what's causing all of this."

Van scoffed. "So, your *i e* what? Recruiting me? You're not serious."

"We've read your research."

"I haven't published anything."

"Imagine that."

"You are validating my inherent fear of strangers."

"Well, I didn't exactly plan for things to go this way."

"Let me guess, dinner, a movie, maybe I'll call you in the

morning…"

"I meant I didn't plan on getting shot."

"Fix what? And how do you know I can fix it? What if I wo—?" There it was again, that sharp, spicy smell, taking over the room like it were a bakery. Van looked up at Cal. "Please tell me you brought cinnamon rolls?"

"What?"

Van staggered backwards, landing against the desk. The sunlight outside faded to darkness and the walls of his office melted away. Suddenly, he wasn't inside, but next door, on the top level of the parking garage, leaning against the back quarter-panel of a car. It was still early morning, just unusually warm, too warm for Van's comfort. At least there was a breeze. He inhaled deeply, filling his lungs with damp, salty ocean air. The smell calmed his nerves and settled his stomach. It was hearty and tinged with … gunpowder … and blood? Van looked to his right. His arm was outstretched; his eyes trailed from his shoulder, to the crook of his elbow, down to his hand and the smoking gun cradled in his palm. At his feet lay a dead man.

He hoped it wasn't Cal. Sort of.

Then, he collapsed.

2

Sunlight pelted Van's face. He turned on his side, pulled the comforter up high over his shoulders and buried his head in the pillow. The linens were soft against his bare skin and the bed was so warm and … so not his. He bolted upright and immediately cracked his head off the ceiling.

"That looked like it hurt. Good morning." A woman stood across the room, leaning against the doorframe. Van noticed the gun holstered to her hip first, then the tightly cut suit that hugged her sylphlike frame. She had shoulder-length black hair, snowy skin and a distinctly Irish brogue.

"How are you feeling?" she asked.

Confused. "Fine," he said. "Do we know each other?"

She shook her head. "I'm Riley, Riley Barnes."

"I see," Van said. "Pleasure to meet you." He shifted around a bit in the bed. He was about to try and get up when he realized that he wasn't wearing a shirt. Or pants.

He looked at Riley. "I'm naked?"

She nodded. "Your clothes are in the bathroom."

"Oh, okay."

She stood, silent, watching while Van tried to figure out what was happening. He looked at the floor, at the ceiling. Keeping the comforter secure, he swung his feet over the edge of the bed. "One more thing. Am I on a boat?"

She smiled. "Join us on deck when you get dressed."

When she left, Van pushed himself from the bed and retrieved his shirt and pants from the bathroom. After dressing, he went up a flight of stairs just outside his stateroom and found himself in the galley. He crossed through, into the saloon and out onto the deck. The sunlight nearly knocked him over. He shielded his eyes and took another set of stairs up to the pilothouse. Cal sat in the Captain's chair.

"Top of the morning to you," he said. "Or it would've been. It's noon." Cal looked him over. His faced turned harsh. "How much do you remember?"

Van thought about it for a minute. "I remember the hospital and you and the morgue and… why aren't you dead again?"

"You were dead?" Riley asked.

Cal ignored her. "That's it?"

"I remember the rapidly rising sun." He plopped down on a bench. "I remember everything. Sort of. Did I shoot someone?"

"He jumped us in the parking garage, when we were leaving. You don't remember any of that?"

"It's all a little hazy. Something happened, in the office. I skipped… ahead."

"You were cognizant of time shifting?" Riley asked.

"Riley is our chief investigator," Cal said. "She's also a theoretical physicist." Van cocked his eyebrows. Riley smiled at him. Beautiful, smart and carries a gun. He was intrigued.

"I feel hung over."

"Most people don't even notice the effects of a break," Cal said.

"Where are we going? And did I choose to come willingly?" Van asked.

"You did."

"We're going to see the craft," Riley said.

Van turned and looked out the portal behind him. "Another boat?"

She shook her head. "No. Not a floating one, anyway."

"It's underwater?"

"Embedded in a canyon, in the deep ocean."

"How'd it get there?"

"It crashed. January 23, 1854."

"Crashed? You mean sunk."

"No, she means crashed," Cal said.

"Did we even have planes back then?"

"No. Our first flight wasn't until 1903," Riley said. She shifted in her seat. "Theirs was probably a lot earlier."

"Theirs, who?"

Riley and Cal exchanged a quick look. Then, finally: "The aliens who built it."

Van assumed Cal and Riley had really brought him out to the middle of the ocean to kill him. That was the only plausible explanation. Aliens? They were screwing with him. Having a little fun before shooting him in the head and dumping his body over the side of the yacht. He was exhausted and disheveled and completely coherent thoughts eluded him. He considered for a moment that he could really be at home in bed, dreaming. Or maybe in a coma somewhere? Maybe he'd been in a horrible accident and this was his subconscious, broken mind acting out as he lay in some hospital bed in a vegetative state? No, he'd never been that lucky.

Ten minutes later, Cal slowed the engine as they passed a series of markers warning of dangerous currents. Eventually, they came to a stop, bobbing up and down as the ocean waves gently rocked the boat. Abruptly, they started sinking. Van jumped from his seat, but Riley assured him it was fine. He looked out the portal and saw, unbelievably, that the surface of the water had split around them and that they were lowering into some kind of under water dry dock.

"Who the hell are you people?" Van asked.

Once the boat had settled onto the docking moors, a pair of glass doors slid closed above them as water poured over the top, concealing the dock and everything in it under the ocean. Cal led them out onto the deck, then across a short gangplank to the docking side. The bay could've held another boat twice the size of the one they'd come on. It even had a helipad.

When Cal's feet hit the docking side, the whole place snapped to life: lights low along the walls faded up and a series of glass monitors hanging around the perimeter came on. In the far wall, a large, round door opened as Cal approached. Van took it for some kind of airlock.

"We all carry one of these," Riley said. She showed him a clear, rectangular piece of glass, about the size and thickness of a cell phone, that she pulled from her pocket. "There's a near-field communication chip inside that controls locking mechanisms and power sources for our systems. We call it a comm."

"You two coming?" Cal called, from inside the airlock.

"Come on," Riley said. "You haven't seen anything yet."

Van hesitated.

"Where's your sense of adventure?" Cal asked.

"Beaten to death by my sense of survival."

"It's perfectly safe."

"Says the man who died in my ER last night."

"I guess you'll just have to trust us."

Van rolled his eyes. He crossed the dock and followed Riley and Cal into the airlock. As he did, the door behind him sealed shut. Cal led them to a small submersible connected at the other end, what Riley called "the lift." After waiting a moment for the air pressures to equalize, Cal opened the outer door, and they all climbed aboard. He sealed them in, released the locking clamps and sent them sinking into the depths of the Pacific.

Van's heart pounded. His hands grew sweaty, and he felt hot. He gripped the armrests of his seat and reminded himself to breathe. When he looked up, Riley was staring.

"You okay?"

"It's a little small in here, that's all."

"Won't be long."

Van settled back in his seat and tried to picture himself on a big, breezy beach, wide open in every direction. It didn't work. He concentrated on his breathing. Riley turned to look out the window beside her, then motioned for Van to come have a look. Slowly, he moved from his bench to hers. She put her hand on his shoulder and pointed out the window. Outside, he saw some faint spots of light slowly fade up out of the dark. As they floated closer, the outlines of the ship's hull came into focus. It was a haphazard conglomeration of stone pillars, boxes and spires caught between the two canyon walls, as Cal had said. Bright, purple circles of light radiated from at least a hundred spots along the hull, casting a haze around the ship. It looked like a spiky Christmas tree ornament.

Eventually, the lift slowed and attached itself to another air lock on the side of the ship. Cal said it would just take a few minutes for the pressures to equalize so they could open the door. "We experimented in the 80s with an elevator-like tube from the upper platform, but it kept cracking and once, an entire research team died. We scrapped it and stuck with the airlock and lift ever since. Before that, the only access had been by submarine," he said.

When the doors finally opened, a rush of cold air smacked Van in the face. It was stale, like an old tomb. He stepped forward and peered out into the darkness, overcome by a sense of ever expanding space.

Cal placed his palm on the wall of the corridor. Immediately, a series of glowing symbols grew around his hand, in the wall and in the air. Then, lights in the ship popped on, one after the other, revealing a network of winding bridges lowering and rising gently from the outer hull throughout belly of the ship. Save a twisted, jagged pillar that rose through the center space and all the way to the top — it looked as if it had been grown instead of built — there weren't any walls. Rock from the sea canyon jutted through the hull in several places.

One of the bridges connected the airlock to the center pillar, near the top. They made their way across and Cal opened a door at the other end by again placing his hand on an innocuous spot on the wall.

"We can access most of the pillar," Riley said, "but the hull didn't seal around the edges of the rock in all places, so many of the lowest decks are flooded."

They stepped into a maze of corridors and stairwells that led downward. Gravity seemed to be an afterthought — at times it felt like they were walking upside down above floors they'd just crossed, and up walls that rose high to the ceiling. Riley remarked that it was a lot like walking on a Möbius strip, as if Van was supposed know what that was. Eventually, they arrived outside a large, hangar-sized door somewhere near the center of the pillar. Cal hit a few controls on the wall and the door slid open with just the small sound of air whooshing from behind it.

Inside, the room was dark and empty, except for a white sphere with glassy walls sitting dead center. It stretched a good forty feet in all directions, so high that its top edges faded into the dark.

"The break, what happened at the hospital. It was all because of this?"

"It's a singularity," Riley said. "A rupture in the fabric of spacetime that occurs in the center of a black hole. The sphere is a kind of containment unit, for lack of a better description. They used it as a power source."

"There's a black hole in that sphere?" He wasn't so much asking, he just wanted to hear himself say it out loud. A black hole? He didn't understand how that was even possible.

"Its presence here has a destabilizing effect on spacetime, which you saw quite a bit of last night," Riley said.

"It breaks time?" Van asked.

"And space. The two are quite intertwined."

"Can we go inside?"

"No," Cal said.

"Why not?"

"Because no one who's ever gone in there has ever come back. But we can show it to you."

He put his hand in the air and a bright set of controls appeared, morphing around his arm. As he manipulated them, the white of the containment unit's walls faded away, revealing a nebulous orb, the size of a billiard ball, hovering inside. The air bent around it like elastic, rippling as though someone had dropped a marble in a still pond. It was a void, so dark that Van's eyes got lost in its center.

"The containment unit is cracked on the upper-left side. It's microscopic, about six feet long, and it's the source of all our problems. Massive amounts of temporal energy escape through it, and that's why you're here."

"Me?"

"The sphere is unlike anything we've ever seen. It's made of some kind of bioneural fiber, a lot like our nervous system. The cells are interlocking, striated and they communicate with each other," he said.

"Like neurons?" From the look on their faces, Van could tell he was oversimplifying, but they both nodded nonetheless. Now everything made a little more sense. "You want me to fix it."

"Nothing we've tried has worked," Cal said. "You're our best hope."

"Best hope?"

"The treatments you're developing could be applicable."

"They don't work."

"We can help with that."

Van shook his head. "What you're talking about isn't... I'm not even board certified yet. I'm less than a year out of residency. There are hundreds of other people more qualified—"

"You are uniquely qualified," Cal said.

"Look, I went into neurology with a theory about neural regeneration that no one else really shares and I work in an ER because it gives me easy access to the population I want to study … but it's just a theory. Even with my research, we're years, maybe decades away from being able to repair this kind of damage and that's assuming this stuff is as much like our nervous system as you're saying."

"We don't have decades," Cal said.

"We probably don't even have years," Riley added.

"You guys are acting like the fate of the world depends on it."

Cal and Riley looked at each other, and then back at Van.

"Oh, man," he said. "Does the fate of the world depend on it?"

"This is a lot to absorb. Just take it slow, okay?"

"What else have you tried?"

"EM field can disrupt the temporal energy, but truthfully,

until we found you, our best plan was to blow the damn thing up," Cal said.

"Blow it up?"

"Well, it wasn't that simple," Riley said. "When you reduce the singularity to its mathematical representation, it becomes clear that a massive energy charge could upend the equation and, as the theory goes, dissolve the event horizon."

"You were going to blow it up."

"Okay, maybe it is that simple."

"What stopped you?"

"I stopped us," Cal said.

Van turned back toward the singularity. Its edges pulsed and blurred, like it were angry.

was

Then, it flashed.

Van found himself standing back at the entrance to the outer room. Cal was still explaining why they couldn't go inside the containment unit with the singularity. Then they were walking toward the door, from the opposite direction. Then he was again standing in front of the containment unit. Then he was back at the door, but also in front of the singularity. Then at the door, in front the singularity and back on the lift, all at once.

Finally, he was looking up at Riley and Cal from the floor. Riley's comm now had a serious of glowing, touch-sensitive buttons. Her fingers flew across the glass as she scanned him.

"What the hell was that?" he asked.

"I'm not sure," Riley said. "You're phasing. But don't worry, it's starting to calm now. You'll be fine." She didn't sound confident.

"Phasing?" His voice almost squeaked. "If I end up embedded in some sea rock I'm gonna kick both your asses."

"Van, what did you see?" Cal asked.

"A lot of stuff. Didn't it— didn't it happen to you?"

Cal shook his head. Van slowly pushed himself up to a sitting position and they helped him to his feet. "Why's it picking on me?"

"It doesn't work that way," Cal said. "The slightest variable can alter the entire course of a break." He hit some buttons on the floating control panel and the containment unit turned solid white again.

"Does it always knock you on your ass like that?"

"I don't know, I've never seen it do that."

"Never?"

Cal shook his head. Van looked at Riley. She shook her head, too.

"I'm ready to go," he said.

Back on land, the sky had turned red as the sun set. Van followed Riley and Cal up the dock and to a parking garage, where a car, the black SUV he'd remembered from the hospital, waited. It smelled awful, like a dead body.

"What is that?" Van asked, crinkling his nose.

"Dead body."

Well, that explained it. "You put him in your car?"

"You're the one who shot him. What was I supposed to do?"

Van shrugged. Cal had a point. He climbed in and rolled down his window. Cal and Riley did the same. "Trust me, you're never getting this smell out," Van said.

They drove south, down the number 5 freeway. It was a short trip, but Van dozed along the way. He roused fully when they pulled into the garage of a high rise on Broadway Avenue, downtown.

"I thought this building was empty," he said.

"That's the point."

Cal parked the car and then led them from the garage through a series of cinder-block corridors. Eventually, they arrived at a set of beige doors, which opened into a slick, marble-lined lobby lit so brightly its walls glowed. And walls they were, stretching a good twenty feet floor to ceiling, towering over a lone guard. His attention was divided among thirty or so flat-screen surveillance monitors suspended form the ceiling. Beyond him, a turnstile guarded a vestibule with two elevators.

Van followed Cal and Riley across the lobby, through the turnstile and into one of the elevators. It carried them so high into the building his ears popped. When the elevator finally stopped, the doors opened and they stepped out into a window-less atrium, four, maybe five stories high.

"Welcome to Station One, Van."

"Station One?"

"We were the first of what President Wilson feared would become many, if more crashed ships were discovered."

"And?"

"So far, so good. Though we did build a fallback bunker in Los Angeles. Just in case."

The upper floors faded into the darkness, but the lower, a series of uneven, terraced platforms, was illuminated by a half-dozen glowing panels, suspended at various angles on wires from the ceiling. Three glass walls, computer consoles, rose from the floor seven or eight feet high and snaked around the edges of the central platform. Several of the outer platforms were basins, overflowing with water into a pool that wrapped around the control center like a moat.

"Water filtration system," Cal said. "The building is designed to be self-sufficient. Plus it's pretty. There's a lab complex below us and several large holding bays in the sub-basements, below the garage." He pointed above them, to a walkway on the second level that wrapped around the atrium. "Your office will be up there, with the rest of the senior staff." As Van's eyes adjusted, he saw catwalks connecting the opposite sides of the higher levels, but no walkways around the perimeter.

"Sickbay is on the third, with our conference rooms. Sleep quarters on the fourth."

"This building is at least 50 stories high, what's below us?"

"Empty floors mostly, security buffers," said a familiar voice, from behind them. Van turned to see Dr. Compton coming down a set of metal-framed stairs from the second level.

"Dr. Compton? What the hell are you doing here?"

"Actually," Cal said. "This is Ben Lindey. He works for me."

"Ben… He what?"

"About eight months ago, when you came on our radar as a possible recruit, I assigned him to the hospital to watch you."

"Are you out of your minds?" He turned to Ben. "You impersonated a doctor?"

"What? It's not like I was performing surgery."

"Well, there was that one time," Cal said. "But I talked to

him about it and he promised to never do it again."

"Sure did."

They were joking. Van hoped, anyway. Surely.

"Oh, and let me introduce you to Walter," Cal said. "Walter, say hello to Dr. Jacobs." *extra space?*

"Hello Dr. Jacobs. May I call you Van?" The voice came from everywhere. It was crisp and rich, almost too perfect. Van glanced around for its source.

"Walter's our mainframe," Cal said. "If you need anything, he can usually help."

"So, how was the field trip?" Ben asked.

"Illuminating," Van said. "Fascinating, even." He turned to Cal. "The tours have been great, but, what if I say no? What are you going to do with me?"

Cal shrugged. "I'll take you home."

"Just like that?"

Cal nodded.

"And what if I try to tell someone about all this?"

"You won't."

"What if I did?"

"You wouldn't want to."

"Fine. Take me home."

"Okay," Cal said.

"Okay? That's it? You went to all this effort, got shot and you don't even look disappointed."

"You got shot?" Ben asked.

"Just a little."

"He died," Van said.

"Really?"

"Van, I am disappointed. But I'm not going to keep you here against your—"

An alarm blared. The soft lighting went down, replaced by an eerie red glow whose source Van couldn't find. In the middle of the control center, a holographic map of San Diego appeared with a pulsating dot near the airport.

"Another break?" Riley asked. She seemed genuinely surprised. She crossed to the control center and checked some readings on a computer screen. "Kascinzki fold. Walter, probability of incursion?"

"Sixty-eight percent and set to rise, Riley."

"Shit," Cal said. He took off for the control platform. Van and Ben followed after him.

"Incursion?" Van asked.

"Remember I told you spacetime can be ripped, torn and folded in any number of ways? Well this break is a fold — it's bringing two points of space that are normally separated together. Sometimes that means that things can... come through where they meet. Things from other places."

"Like what? Like, aliens?"

Cal nodded.

"So what do you do?"

"Most of the time, they don't survive the transition, for whatever reason. The ones that do we classify. Class ones are microscopic, like viruses, bacteria. Class twos are small, small like say, dogs. They get bigger from there."

"You kill them?"

Cal looked at Ben, then back at Van. "If it comes to that, yes. At least, we do now, anyway."

"Now?"

"Well… If they were benign, and say, class twos, or something smaller, we've been known to let them go."

"Let them go? Like to — to live here?"

"Sometimes, yeah. I mean we used to. Not so much anymore."

"Like what?"

He sighed. "You know… microscopic bacteria and phages and things you'd never even know where there unless we told you."

"Oh. That's okay, I guess."

"Well, if you think West Nile Virus is okay," Ben said.

"What?"

"Ben, shut up," Cal said.

"And sea lions," Ben said.

"Sea lions?"

"Ben!"

"Sea lions are aliens?"

Cal sighed, then nodded.

"You're lying."

"Really not. But like I said, we don't do that anymore. Not since I've been here. It involved a lot of falsifying records and creating fake fossils and lying to the CDC… anyway, these days the Internet makes it a lot harder. People are much smarter."

"What else are aliens?"

Cal turned and looked at Van. "You don't want to know," he said.

Van was about to protest when Riley interrupted to say she'd localized the break. "Fantastic," Cal said. "Take Van."

"What? No, that's… no."

"Nonsense," Riley said. "It'll be fun."

"I've had enough fun. Just take me home."

"That'll have to wait until this is all over, now. It could be a few hours," Cal said.

Van sighed, long and hard. Had he not known better, he would've assumed Cal had planned this.

"You're not even a little bit curious about what's out there?" Ben asked, as he slipped on his suit jacket.

"I know what you guys are trying to do," Van said.

"Manipulate you?"

"Yes."

"Is it working?"

"Little bit."

"Stay close to these two," Cal said. "Do what they say."

Van nodded. Once they were back in the elevator, he turned to Riley: "So, what is it? Will it be big?"

"Nah. The break was relatively small," she said. "Nothing like what you experienced last night. We'll be lucky if this is even a class one. Probably won't notice a thing."

Riley was right about the break on one count: it was nothing like he'd experienced the night before. But she was very wrong about them not noticing a thing. Van could tell from the moment they'd arrived that things were probably very noticeable. The break occurred between Old Town and the airport, an industrial space filled with a lot of warehouses and factories. It was easy to spot the problem. One of the warehouses was surrounded by people, ambulances and fire trucks.

"What are the police doing here?" Riley asked. She directed the question to no one in particular, but Van thought it was a good one that deserved answers. *an answer?*

"I thought you said we we'd barely notice anything?"

"It's not an exact science, you know. More like a hazy estimation."

"Obviously, something's drawn a lot of attention," Van said.

Ben called back to Station to ask Cal to get in touch with their liaison in the police department. It was a few more minutes before the command sergeant on scene, a hulking African America with biceps the size of cannons, begrudgingly escorted them behind the police tape. He stared at Ben the entire time. Van guessed he wasn't used to taking orders from a considerably *→ extra space?* skinnier white guy, let alone one half his age and wearing a suit with a hipster-thin tie.

"How many are still inside?" Ben asked.

"At least seven unaccounted for," the sergeant said.

"We've got it from here. Move your perimeter back."

He didn't. Instead, he stood fast and folded his arms across his chest.

"Maybe you didn't hear me?" Ben asked.

The sergeant dropped his arms to his sides, snatched one of the nearby police barriers and then tossed it down the road at least fifty feet. "That far enough?"

Ben nodded. "That'll do."

The building's door was on the far side, opposite the parking lot and facing the roadway. They left the sergeant to stew, and made their way around until they came to the entrance. It hung open.

"Looks dark in there," Van said.

"Perhaps the power has failed," Riley said.

Van looked up. Like most of the other warehouses, this one had a clerestory that ran the entire length of the roof. It was facing west into the setting sun.

"Right, the power's just out."

They stepped inside. It took a few seconds for Van's eyes to adjust, but nothing looked amiss. Palettes stacked with boxes, forklifts idling, conveyor belts still rolling. It was almost anticlimactic.

"So what now?" he asked.

Before anyone could answer, the building shuddered from the top down. They looked to the ceiling, and all saw it at the same time: an amorphous, black blob spread across the rafters and down most of the west wall.

"That is not barely noticeable!" Van shouted.

"In my defense," Riley said, "it probably was fairly small when it passed through the break, judging from the rate that it's growing."

"Is it alive?" Van asked.

"Looks that way," Ben said.

"Is it going to eat us?"

He nodded. "Probably."

3

Seventeen seconds went by without anyone moving, talking. That was seventeen too many for Van. He yelled for Ben and Riley to do something as the building heaved under the weight of the alien blob spreading across its ceiling. Riley scanned the area with her comm.

"I've got five human life signs — over there." She pointed to a small room built out on the factory floor. Parts of the alien had run down over top of it, blocking its door.

"Are they hurt?" Van asked.

"It's not that specific."

"How do we get them out?"

"We make a new door," Ben said.

Riley pointed to the far wall. "They're huddled in a corner on the other end. That's the safest point."

Ben nodded. "Okay, go tell the Incredible Hulk out there that this whole place is about to come down and to get everyone as far back as he can." Riley looked uncertain about leaving them, but did as she was told.

Ben and Van ran across the warehouse floor, some two hundred feet, to the room where the workers were trapped. The building moaned as its metal frame buckled. Van pushed the noise to the back of his mind and tried to focus on what Ben was doing. He'd attached a small, circular disk — it looked like a piece of a mylar balloon — to the part of the wall Riley had indicated. Then, he grabbed Van by the elbow and pulled him back behind a palette of boxes.

"What is that thing?" Van asked. He peered around the edge of the palette, just as Ben pressed a button on his comm. The disc exploded, tearing a hole in the wall. Before Van could even get his bearings, Ben was across the floor and yelling at the workers inside to run for the exit. Then, he screamed for Van. They climbed through the hole together and found an older guy, maybe sixty, in a dirty jump suit and sprawled out on the floor. Blood covered his face.

"Can we move him?"

"If the alternative is being buried under this building, I'd say yes. Help me," Van said. They hoisted him up on their shoulders and started for the exit. As they moved, the guy roused. "Can you walk? *¿Puedes caminar?*"

The man's eyes met Van's, and then he looked up at the ceiling. He saw the alien, broke from their arms and took off half running, half-hobbling for the door.

"I guess that's a yes."

"Let's get out of here."

They were too late.

The wall around the exit caved, burying the hobbling man and sealing Ben and Van inside. Behind them, the ceiling fell, sending masses of wood, metal and alien hurling like a tidal wave. They ran for the other side of the warehouse, but there were no doors in sight, not even a fire exit.

They turned, backs pressed, to face what was coming. The blob hit the ground in a whoosh, propelled their way by the collapsing ceiling. Van braced himself for a collision, but instead, the alien popped like a balloon, splattering everything. Released, the building settled and the collapse slowed, stopping just short of burying them.

Van looked down at himself. Exploded alien covered him from his face to the pair of tennis shoes he'd bought just last week. He reached up and tried, fairly unsuccessfully, to wipe his eyes and mouth. The goo was sticky, warm. Gritty.

"I know I haven't known you guys very long," he said. "But I hate you, a lot."

It'd been years, well into medical school, before Van had gotten used to the rotten smell of blood; dried alien guts was going to take a lot longer. Riley helped them crawl from the wreckage and when Cal arrived on scene, he sent them back to Station to clean up.

"You reek of death and sewer," he said.

When they arrived at Station One, Ben showed him to a

locker room on a deck below the operations level. There was a fit-ness center down the hall, Ben said, but Van couldn't have cared less. He stripped off his clothes, tossed them in a wastebasket and headed for the shower. He cranked up the water and stepped under the spray, letting out a long sigh as the water peeled away the slime. He was on his third scrub down when Ben came in and stepped under one of the shower heads across from him.

"So this is a typical work day?" Van asked.

"More or less. Usually more."

Dried alien caked Ben's face and neck like a mud mask, but he stood underneath the water as though he was taking a leisure-ly shower after a weekend nap. Van's approach was the opposite, just short of a vigorous delousing. Actually, he wondered if they had any delousing powder?

"I put some clothes out on the bench for you," Ben said. Van had finished rinsing, but decided it wouldn't hurt to shampoo his hair once more. "I know this is a lot to take, especially as fast as it's all come at you. Thank Cal for that, he doesn't believe in dipping your toes. Likes to throw people in the deep end and see if they can swim."

"What happens if I drown?"

"What's bothering you the most?"

"You know, I was on board with the whole rupturing space-time thing. But... I don't know."

"Aliens?"

"Yeah."

"You saw it."

"It's not that I don't believe it. It's just..."

"Foundation shaking."

"Yeah, I guess."

"You a religious guy, Van?"

"You've been spying on me for the last eight months, you tell me."

He laughed. "I'm just saying religious types don't like the basic premise. We're not alone. Everything we know is wrong. Reality is more than what we see and hear and feel. Our human minds aren't exactly equipped to deal with those ideas."

Van stopped cleaning himself long enough to take that in. "What goes on in those distant depths…," he said. Ben looked at him curiously. Van shook his head, and then changed the subject. "Riley's mind seems equipped for it."

"Yeah, well, just don't get her started on elementary particles. She loves those."

"Thanks for the tip."

"So, why does a doctor join the CIA?"

"Officially, I didn't."

Ben smiled. "Okay, unofficially."

Van shrugged. "You want me to boil it down? Why'd you join Station One? I don't know, it seemed like the best way — unofficially — to make a difference, I guess. That's corny. Is that corny? Doesn't matter anyway, I scrubbed out."

"No you didn't. You quit. There's a difference."

"Not from my perspective."

Ben turned his water off. "There are a few sleeping quarters upstairs, if you want to try and get some rest until Cal gets back. Then he can take you home." He grabbed a towel off the rack just outside the shower but before leaving, turned back. "And Van?"

"Yeah?"

"Maybe, I don't know, this is the second best way some-one could make a difference, unofficially." He wrapped the towel around his waist and walked off.

Twelve hours and thirty-three minutes later, Van bolted upright, sweating and panting. He'd been having a nightmare, probably, but whatever it was had faded fast. He looked around, confused at first. Then it all came rushing back: the night at the hospital, the two dead men (only one of whom was still dead), the alien ship, the exploding blob. He groaned and rubbed his eyes. He'd meant to sleep for just an hour. He looked down at himself. Ben had left him a pair of baggy grey sweatpants and a white un-dershirt that looked like it probably came in a pack of six from Target. Not exactly his style — and no shoes, either.

Barefoot, he groped in the darkness until he found his way out onto the third floor of the operations center. He stepped up to the railing and looked down to the first level, where Ben and Riley stood talking by one of the large computer walls. He couldn't hear what they were saying from so far up, but they were joking, laughing. Maybe Ben had forgotten about being covered with the insides of an alien just hours before? Van shuddered at the memory.

He made his way down to the second level and found Cal, in his office, watching the news. A city councilwoman, Lynn Zora, was being interviewed about the "earthquake" that leveled a warehouse in her district yesterday. She was promising government aid for the business owners whose enterprise had been shut down. Van heard nothing about plans to also help the hundred or so workers now out of jobs. When Cal noticed Van at the door, he pushed the screen aside, swiveled in his chair and offered him a seat.

"Good morning."

"I can't believe I slept all night."

"Well, you had an explosive day," he said.

"I don't find that funny."

"Everyone survived, save the one elderly gentlemen you tried to help."

"So there's a bright side, then. Sort of."

"They're analyzing the substance you guys were covered with over in the lab, looks to be mostly some basic organic compounds, but..."

"What?"

"The samples we collected are mutating. Quickly."

"So what does that mean?"

"I've got no idea," Cal said. "The lab has synthesized a compound that inhibits its cell growth, though. We think you and Ben should be inoculated, just in case."

"Inoculated?"

Just then, a young woman, Asian and willowy, came through Cal's door carrying a briefcase. She wore a lab coat and rimless glasses with bright red frames.

"Van, this is Anna." She smiled at Van, placed her case on Cal's desk and took out a small contraption that looked too much like a gun for Van's comfort.

"Your arm, please."

Van turned his arm up and laid it across Cal's desk. In one swift move Anna put the gun to the underside of his forearm and pulled the trigger. Van yelped and rubbed the rapidly forming red spot the gun left behind. He glared at Cal.

"Have you tested this on humans?"

"Yeah, just now."

Anna packed her case and left. Van stood to his feet. "You are unbelievable."

"What? You're saying you, of all people, has a problem with pushing the bounds of medical science and ethics?" Cal leaned back in his chair and put his arms behind his head, obviously satisfied with himself. "Relax, it's safe," he said. "Believe it or not, we've had some experience in this area. I'll have a stock supply delivered to your house."

Slowly, Van slunk bank into the chair. "Stock supply? How often do I have to take this stuff?"

"We'll you'd be the expert on that, but the lab's saying… weekly?"

"For how long?"

"We'll let you know."

Van rubbed his arm again. "Stranger danger."

"You ready to go home?"

"I had a whole speech planned here, but then you shot me up with a vaccine that you developed in less than twenty-four hours and that's thrown off my rhythm a bit. Look, this is all kind of nuts. I think you're all completely crazy and I'm still not convinced this isn't some kind of elaborate hoax at my expense — and I reserve the right to change my mind after I'm fully awake and in command of all my mental faculties, but, no, I don't want to go home."

"What do you want?"

He sat silent for a long time, then: "I want on the team."

Cal smiled. "Great. Because I'd already pushed your paper-work through the night before I went to find you at the hospital. Now, do you surf?"

Van imagined talking to Cal wasn't that different than being whiplashed.

"Do I—? Why?"

Van woke early. It was Saturday, the end of a truly unremark-able, even tedious, first week at Station One. Half of it he'd spent locked in the conference room with a lanky Hispanic guy named Carlos. For hours, they poured over every conceivable screen, but-ton and app on Van's comm, in between long treatises on why Carlos's first, second and third marriages failed and why he be-lieved, with all sincerity, that bow ties and vests were the marks of well dressed men. Van listened, smiled and nodded at the ap-propriate times and tried hard to keep his eyes from glazing over.

When he wasn't with Carlos he was in the lab, plowing through Station's research on the containment unit. Riley's de-scription of the material as a kind of nerve fiber was pretty apt, though he spotted some key structural differences in the cells that he didn't really understand. The only clear thing was that the material was made of biological compounds, which meant they'd grown it. Probably. Maybe. He knew nothing. He'd gone home the night before with a headache and an impending sense of death and destruction.

Van rolled out of bed, begrudgingly, showered, then dressed in an old pair of jeans and a T-shirt without really taking the time to dry off. He grabbed a banana on his way out the door and was in his car and on the 8 freeway just as the sun started to rise. Cal hadn't been able to ID the man Van shot when they were leaving the hospital the week before, but he had traced the gun he'd been carrying. It was last registered to one Kyle Owens, prominent San Diego businessman and budding philanthropist. Kyle was — so far as they knew — still alive, and he'd reported the gun stolen two years ago, so it was possible he wasn't involved. Cal wanted to know for sure.

"He's an avid surfer, apparently," Cal had said. "So are you."

"So you want me to …"

"Get close to him. Establish some common ground. He surfs the breaks at Sunset Cliffs with the Point Loma club every Saturday."

Sunset Cliffs wasn't one of Van's favorite spots. The same jagged outcrops that made for great surf made it difficult to get down to the water. There were no steps, just a rocky path. He parked his car at the top along the road and, after slipping into his wet suit, started down to the beach.

The club was loosely formed, it turned out. When Van arrived, he was greeted by an older man with long grey hair. He introduced a few of the other members, and told Van that they usually had a dozen or so show up out of the fifty that called the club home. Van was disappointed when he realized Kyle Owens wasn't among the ones in attendance that Saturday.

They set out as a group, paddling over the breaking waves near the shoreline to find a good holding spot. Van had positioned himself for a wave when he saw a stick-thin blond guy with a blue surfboard jogging toward the water from the path down the cliffs. Even from far out, his grin glared like a road flare. He waved his arms over his head and yelled out to them: "Good morning, y'all!"

Van turned to the old man, who was floating to his left. "Kyle Owens," he said. "Never on time, never without that shit-eating grin. Hope you like morning people."

Van smiled. He hated morning people.

They surfed for about an hour, but Van's stride was off and the surf was rough. He kept missing the waves and the ones he did catch promptly pulled him under and chewed him up. The rest of the group wasn't faring a whole lot better though, so he didn't feel bad. They called it quits around 7:30, a bit early, and began the slow hike back up to their cars.

Van quickly stripped out of his wet suit, using the door to his Prius for privacy. He watched as Kyle Owens, parked a few cars from his, did the same. He was busy estimating the number of Saturday mornings he'd have to spend surfing with the Point Loma club before he could approach Kyle without arousing suspicions, when Kyle shut his car door and started Van's way, smile fully intact. After a vigorous hand shaking and a round of introductions, Kyle said: "I've seen you out here before."

Interesting. Van wouldn't have been able to tell Kyle from any other guy on the beach before he'd seen his picture, but Kyle remembered him? Van looked him over. They were about the same height, but Kyle was rail-thin, his face was gaunt and his

hair so blonde Van would've called it white. He'd pulled on a pair
of jeans and *a* baggy plaid button-up, but hadn't put on any shoes.

"I live just down the road, right here on Sunset Cliffs Boulevard," Kyle said. Van knew that already; Kyle and his wife Katie
had bought their home just five years earlier, a 5,000 *square* foot Mc-
Mansion overlooking the Pacific, for about $8 million. He also
knew Kyle's date of birth, his social security number and the
number of credit lines listed on his credit report. What he didn't
know yet was if Kyle was a murderer.

Van wanted to keep him talking, show an interest, so he
tried hard to find engaging things to discuss, beyond the weather. This was San Diego, it never changed anyway. So, he asked:
How long had Kyle been surfing? Only since he moved from
Alabama. That explained the accent, but the grin was still a mys-
tery. Did he like Sunset Cliffs? No, he much preferred Mission
Beach, but this was closer to home. They talked about living near
the cliffs, the sunrise, the way traffic had picked up on the boulevard lining the coast and how they'd both ended up settling
in San Diego. Van of course lied about that part. Telling people
that you scrubbed out of spy school is generally against the rules.
After a few minutes, they ran out of topics. Kyle gave him a
cheery goodbye and a promise to see him soon. Of that, Van had
no doubt.

Back at Station, Van reviewed his morning at the beach for Cal.
He told him about the surfing, about Kyle being late, about Kyle

being the one to make the first move.

"He wanted to look friendly, I think."

"He seem to buy your cover?"

Van shrugged. "I guess we'll see."

To the outside world, Station One looked like a research and development facility that specialized in coming up with new ways to build advanced textiles. At least, that's what it said on paper. Van was listed as the head of a team that would concentrate on biomedical applications for all kinds of new and exciting fabrics. Sure, it was lame, but it merged well with his medical background, should anyone get really curious.

"You know, if Kyle's one of the guys who came after you, then they made you somehow." *said Van.*

Cal nodded. "It had occurred to me. But they think I'm dead now. That's our advantage." He shuffled some papers. "How's the other work coming?"

"I think I've ready everything Station has produced on the containment unit over the last 100 years."

"That's a start."

"Not really. You guys don't have much."

"True."

"I need to replicate the material, for testing."

"We've tried. It's not worked before."

"I'm going on the assumption that it can be cultured, kind of like crystal. But I have no idea, really."

"I've got faith in you."

"One of us should." He stood. "Now, I'm off to review the staff's medical charts and see who's due for a physical, then finish rewriting the medical protocols. I only got halfway before the week ended."

"It's Saturday, go home."

He shook his head. "Riley's coming in later. She's gonna give me a crash course on quantum physics and string theory."

"Just don't let her go on about elementary particles. You'll regret it."

"Yeah, so I've heard."

Van returned to his office and checked his email. Carlos had sent him some paper he'd picked up at a military symposium in D.C. It was something about weapons research on sound waves, and he wanted Van's medical opinion so he could prepare a report for their weekly briefing. Van filed it away to look at later, then tried to get as much work done as he could before Riley arrived. He finished reviewing the medical charts and then plowed his way through the last half of the medical protocols, noting changes for Cal to approve later. He drew a smiley face next to directive 9.3. That was the one that required a medical doctor on staff at all times, and it also gave him the ability to assume command of Station and its systems if, in his judgment, Cal was mentally or physically incapacitated. He tried to imagine himself giving Cal orders. The thought made him chuckle, just as Riley poked her head in the door.

"Something funny?"

"Probably only to me."

She took a seat, and after a few minutes catching up and hearing about Van's morning at the beach, they started down a path that, two hours later, led to one inevitable conclusion: physics was not Van's strength.

"I'm sorry, I'm not explaining things well at all," Riley said, after valiantly trying to explain the Heisenburg uncertainty principle to him as many different ways as she could.

Van shook his head. "It's not your fault."

She leaned back in her chair. "I know exactly what we need."

"Yeah?"

"Two for one margaritas until 8, at Hurricane, in the Gas Lamp."

Van groaned. "I don't know if I'm in the mood for happy hour."

"How will you know until you try?"

He couldn't argue with that. He logged off his work station, grabbed his blazer and they were off.

The Gas Lamp district wasn't far from Station One. Ben was already at the bar when Van and Riley arrived, along with a few other people Van recognized: Carlos, that young Asian girl who'd given him his shot — what was her name? Ann? Anna? — and a tall guy whose specialty was Xenolinguistics, whatever that was. Van joined Ben in a booth while Riley scooted off to the bar. She came back with three frozen margaritas on a tray, which she sat in front of them. She proposed a toast to Van and a successful first day in the field, and a long, successful tenure as Station's chief medical officer.

"So, no one's told me. What happened to my predecessor?"

Ben took a long swig of his margarita before answering. "He was killed."

Van shrugged. Not that he liked hearing it, but he had figured as much. He gulped his drink. They sat talking about nothing in particular and after a while, Ben excused himself when he spotted someone he knew. Van lost track of him at some point in the evening, only to spot him later in another booth across the room, in very close proximity to a staggeringly pretty Italian guy in a Hugo Boss shirt and Seven for All Mankind jeans.

Van turned to Riley. "So Ben. He's gay?"

She nodded. "He didn't tell you?"

"No, it didn't come up, you know, while we were… showering together."

"Yeah that would seem like the perfect opportunity."

Van thought about that for a few moments, then decided to stop thinking about it. He turned back to Riley. "So tell me about you, Agent Dr. Riley Barnes."

"Oh I'm completely straight."

"I meant, what horribly fascinating chain of events brought you to become part of our little alien monster squad?"

"Cal and I crossed paths when a case I was working in New York brought me here to San Diego. He offered me a job on the spot. It took a lot of convincing, actually. I mean, I thought he was nuts. But he showed me the singularity and one thing led to another and here I am. That was just 13 long, long months ago."

Her face turned down.

"What's wrong?"

"I've been here little more than a year and the singularity is outpacing my projections before I can even figure them. Cal said when he first arrived — maybe ten years ago — they experienced three or four events a year. We're up to thirty and counting, on track to make this year the worst ever."

"Has something changed?"

She shook her head. "All I can really do is forecast its behavior, but not well. It's a lot like predicting an earthquake. One can destabilize spacetime enough to precipitate others. Only... Sometimes, you think you've got an earthquake when all you've really got is the foreshock. The big one is yet to come."

"If the bomb idea was so promising, why did Cal shut it down?"

"Station's ordnance lab is responsible in large part for some of the most devastating weapons the world's ever seen. And then, the last bomb they developed scared the hell out of everyone."

"What kind of bomb?"

"An antimatter device."

"I didn't know we'd discovered antimatter."

"Officially, we have not."

"We have these things, at Station?"

"I've never seen them, but I presume they're secured in the ordnance lab. Cal locked it down when he got here 10 years ago, and no one's been inside it since."

The evening had taken a depressing turn. It was late, and they both planned to be up early the next morning to catch up on work before the weekend ended. Ben had left hours before with the pretty Italian. Before either Van or Riley could leave, though, there was a pressing issue to deal with.

"So you've noticed that guy in the blue T-shirt across the room?" he asked.

Riley nodded. He'd followed them into the bar earlier that evening and had spent the entire night alone, casually glancing

their way every now and then. He'd kept an eye on their move-
ments most of the night. Van hadn't said anything, hoping he'd
get bored and leave, but it looked like he was in this — whatever
"this" was — until the end. "We can lose him if we split up, go
our separate ways," Riley said.

"He'll still be able to follow one of us."

Riley thought on that for a moment. "Then we need a distraction." She handed her purse to Van, slid her way around to
the end of the booth and started across the room to a crowd of
women standing by the bar. Without warning, she tossed her
drink in the face of a particularly shocked young lady who'd been
chatting with her friends.

"Bitch!" Riley shouted. "He was mine!"

Van sat stunned as Riley berated the girl and caused a throng
of chaos around her. She turned to one of the woman's friends.

"You have something to say, whore!?"

Before Van could figure out what was happening, a crowd
had gathered, cutting of the blue shirt's view. Two bouncers
who'd been standing at the front door took Riley by the arms
and dragged her screaming from the bar. Van grabbed his bag
and Riley's coat and purse and followed them out, as fast as he
could.

The bouncers tossed Riley, and the minute she was out the
door, she stopped screaming, thanked the men for their assis-
tance and turned to Van, who still wasn't quite sure to make of it
all. Distraction, indeed.

"Your apartment's to the west, right?"

Van nodded.

"Good, go. Send me a text when you get home. I'm heading

north up to Broadway and then I'll cut over and double back to the parking garage." She glanced back through the door. The bar was still in a bit of chaos. "Hurry, he's going to find his way out of there soon enough."

And with that, she was gone. Van smiled. So, Cal wasn't the only one who was nuts. Good to know.

The man in the blue shirt pushed his way through the bar and out onto the sidewalk. They were gone. He looked up and down the street, but saw only tourists stumbling back to their hotels after long nights of drinking. He cursed under his breath and started fishing in his pockets for his car keys.

"That was smooth, he made you the second you followed us into the bar."

He looked up. Riley had come around the corner and was standing in front him, her arms crossed. She looked angry. The guy shrugged. "Sorry," he said. "I'll do better next time."

She nodded, then turned and walked off down the street.

Cal had told Van that he'd had all the security cameras at the hospital checked the night he was shot. The one just outside the north doors should've captured the shooting, but there was nothing on it when they went back to check the tapes. As the timelines merged, Cal reasoned, the timeline where he didn't get shot was the one that survived on the security footage. Van hadn't understood that completely and he'd spent a good portion of the night tossing in bed, thinking it through again and again. If the timelines had merged, why were the living Cal and the dead Cal both still around?

"A break is like an injury. It heals, but there's scar tissue left behind. Evidence of the break," Riley had said the day before, trying to explain. Whatever. But Van had a thought. If both Cals survived the merge, then maybe other things did too. He remembered an incident last year when some wiring in the server room at the hospital caught fire and destroyed a bunch of computers and their files. Since then, the hospital had been backing up the collective data of all its computers off-site to a remote location. If the DVRs that held the surveillance video had been backed up before the timelines merged, maybe the footage of Cal being shot still existed. He got up early the next morning and went straight to the hospital.

Gordon, one of the security supervisors, looked at Van as if he was crazy when he asked to see the footage.

"I'd consider it a personal favor," Van said.

He'd been working less than two days at the hospital when he, in trying to balance his pager, a cell phone, a can of soda and a tray of lasagna, tripped over a loose shoe lace and dumped his dinner all over Gordon's back. Since then, every time Gordon saw him, he threw his hands in the air and said "Watch out, Dr. Jacobs is coming," with a big smile on his face. Gordon thought that was hilarious.

"I'm sorry Dr. Jacobs, I can't do it. You're not even supposed to be on hospital grounds."

"It's really important."

He shook his head. "If there was any way—"

"How does $1,000 sound?"

"Sounds great. But you know, we looked at everything with the police that night. There's nothing on there."

"Yeah. But I was hoping you could pull the video from the backup servers."

Gordon shrugged. "Yeah, I guess I could. What's the point?"

"I'm hoping we'll find out."

Gordon took a few minutes, but found the backups he was looking for. "It'll take just a few seconds to download. Here." He got up and let Van take his chair. The files were saved in chunks, so Van had to scrub through more than an hour until he found what he was looking for. Just before 12 a.m., Cal appeared on the screen. So did the man who shot him.

"That's not Kyle Owens," Cal said. They'd gathered on the operations level with Ben and Riley to watch the footage Van had found. Van shook his head. It wasn't Kyle Owens.

"But obviously, there's some connection. It was Kyle's gun," Riley said.

Cal replayed his last few seconds over and over, watching himself get shot again and again. Finally, he turned back to Van. "So how are things going with Mr. Sunshine?"

"Well, as luck would have it I ran into Kyle and his wife Katie at the grocery store this morning, after I went to the hospital."

"They shop at your grocery store?" Ben asked.

"No, but I'm shopping at theirs, for the time being."

"What's Katie Owens like?" Riley asked.

"Young, excruciatingly bubbly, same maniacal smile. They invited me to a party Kyle's throwing for his clients at their palatial mansion on the coast, Thursday night."

"That was fast," Ben said.

"They're friendly to a fault. And they said I could bring a date." He looked at Riley.

"Perfect," Cal said. "You two can be a couple."

"Wait, what?" Ben asked.

"Something wrong?" Cal asked.

"First, you send him surfing, now to a party?

"What's the problem?"

"Maybe Van's priorities shouldn't be so divided right now. I mean, is this really the most important thing he could be—"

"Yes!" Cal snapped. Ben fell silent. Van looked at Riley, but she'd turned her gaze to the floor. Cal turned to Van. "Come up with a cover story about how the two of you met. Spend some time on it. I'm serious."

Then, he turned and stormed off. Ben and Riley shuffled away, too, neither saying a word.

Thursday evening, as they walked to the front door of the Owens' house, Riley turned to Van and asked "So, how'd we meet?"

Van shrugged. "At a bar?"

"Works for me."

They'd spent the days since Sunday working together in the lab, trying to replicate the neural fibers that made up the containment unit. Their first attempts didn't even crystallize and the ones that did were so fragile they shattered if someone spoke too loudly or the air conditioning blew too hard. They were missing something, and after four days of trying, they weren't any closer to figuring out what that something was. By the time Thursday rolled around, Van was looking forward to some time in the field, especially some time in the field with Riley.

She wore a sleeveless black dress with a high waist, and her clutch sparkled in the moonlight. She'd put on makeup and pulled her hair up into an elegant braid. Van's heart had fluttered a bit when she walked out of her house earlier in the evening. He'd gotten some of the shag cut out his hair earlier in the afternoon and a sports coat dry-cleaned for the occasion, but he had to keep reminding himself that it wasn't actually a real date.

He rang the doorbell, and Katie answered. She wore pearls, camel-colored high heels and a regal, cashmere suit jacket and skirt; her smile was so forced Van was sure it'd taken Botox to fix the muscles in that position. Looking her over, he flashed on Laura Bush, sans 30 or 40 years.

"You made it," Katie squealed. "And who is this lovely young thing?" Riley extended her hand and introduced herself, but Katie stepped in and gave her a hug instead. Riley grimaced, but held her composure. "Come on in, come on in," Katie said. "We're just so thrilled you all could make it tonight. We throw a party like this every couple of months for Kyle's clients. Keeps them happy, you know?"

"What business is your husband in?" Riley asked.

"He's a consultant."

"Everyone's outside on the patio," Katie said, as she led them through the entryway, then the main living space, the dining room and the chef's kitchen, all on the first floor. Huge windows stretched from floor to ceiling, providing a stunning view of the coast. Whatever kind of consulting Kyle Owens did, it kept him living in style.

The patio, a multi-level terrace, surrounded a pool and small grotto. They'd strung Chinese lanterns throughout the gardens and wrapped the palm trees with thousands of twinkling lights. An impressive number of people milled about, some sitting around one of the many fire rings, others lounging by the pool, and even more gorging themselves at the spread of *hors d'oeuvres* and open bar.

Kyle spotted them as soon as they stepped outside. He called out from across the patio and came nearly running to greet them. After a round of introductions between he and Riley, he led them from the bar to the food tables, then, it seemed, to meet every other person at the party. Van was nearing his limit on introductions, fake smiles and handshakes when Kyle dragged them up to a group of middle-aged men and women talking near the terrace's edge. He immediately picked one of the men out of the crowd and introduced him first.

"This is the Reverend Charles Sinclair, pastor at First Christian Church here in Point Loma," Kyle said. They didn't need an introduction, though. Van recognized the portly, curly-haired man as the guy on the surveillance video he'd retrieved at the hospital. It was the same guy who'd shot and killed Cal.

4

Holding his breath, Van extended his hand to the Reverend Charles Sinclair, watching closely for any signs that he'd been recognized. He'd hate to have to shoot someone in front of all these party guests. Sinclair met Van's hand and shook, a smarmy grin spread across his face.

"Nice to meet you, young man." He turned toward Riley. "And this pretty lady is…"

"Riley, Riley Barnes," she said.

"Ah, Irish, are you? I spent a semester in Dublin during seminary."

"Lovely. I'm from Arklow myself."

Kyle introduced the rest of the group, whose names Van barely caught, while Sinclair went back to admiring his drink and chatting with a brunette in a matronly dress standing beside him. Van eyed the minister carefully. He'd prepared for a lot of contingencies in his mind, but this wasn't one of them.

"Van, did you hear me?"

Kyle was talking. Reluctantly, Van turned to face him. "I'm sorry, lost in thought."

"I was just saying there are a few more guests I'd like for you to meet..."

"May I use your bathroom, first?"

"Well sure, it's inside at the top of the stairs."

Riley touched him on the elbow. "You feeling all right, honey?" He turned to look at her. Her eyes said something totally different. "You know, I could use a little freshening up, myself. Will you all excuse us?" She took Van by the arm and led him inside.

"What do we do?" Van asked.

Riley looked back out at the party, through one of the windows in the hallway. "He doesn't look as though he's recognized you. You said yourself you wouldn't have recognized him even if the two of you had crossed paths at the hospital."

A couple came in behind them, down the hallway, laughing and giggling and tripping over themselves. Riley led Van toward the front of the house, out of earshot. "What do you want to do?" she asked.

"We need to find the gun that actually shot Cal. We need to tie the Owens and Sinclair to the shooting, definitively."

Riley frowned. "You want to go traipsing about their house?"

"We might never get another chance."

She nodded. "I'll go back to the party and keep them talking. Move quickly, be back out there in five minutes or I'm coming back to collect you."

Riley left and Van, and after a quick glance to make sure no one was watching, he turned and headed up the stairs. The first room he came to looked like a guest bedroom. But at the end of the upstairs hall, he found Kyle's den. The door wasn't locked when he tried the handle, so he slipped inside and shut the door. He tried to make quick work of scanning Kyle's bookshelves and rifling through the files in his cabinets. Nothing stood out.

Then, he came across an envelope filled with canceled checks, all made out to the Reverend Sinclair's church. The amounts varied, but were always under $10,000, probably to avoid triggering automatic alerts to the government. Those transactions hadn't shown up in the bank records Cal had gotten, so they must have been drawn on an account they didn't yet know about. Van used his comm to scan the account and routing numbers on the bottom of one of the checks, and then did the same for the church's endorsement stamp on the back.

He glanced around at the room. There was a closet on the other side he hadn't opened yet. Before he could get there, though, the handle on the door to the den clicked. He dove to the ground, then scrambled to get himself hidden underneath Kyle's desk. He held his breath and prepared for a fight, but instead, he heard Riley whisper his name. He peeked out from behind the desk.

"You scared the hell out of me."

"Sorry." She closed the door quietly.

"I thought you were distracting the Owens?"

"They're distracted. The good reverend is regaling everyone with stories of his time as a missionary in the heathen jungles of Africa."

Van opened the closet, but inside all he found was a door-sized safe with an electronic lock. He took out his comm and tried to recall his training sessions with Carlos. After a few fumbling attempts, he found the app that could brute force the pass code by analyzing the wear and tear on the keys. It took a couple dozen tries before it hit on the right code, but eventually the locks released and the door swung open.

"That's an awful lot of knives and guns for a business consultant," Riley said.

"Maybe he works in the rough part of town?"

"Are those grenades?"

"God, doesn't this guy have a garage? Who keeps explosives in their home office?"

"Maybe he's hoping for a tax deduction?"

In among the bombs, the swords, the knives, the semi-automatic guns, a stack of files and some old, worn books sat on a shelf. Van stepped in, picked out the thickest one and read the spine.

"What's *Coram Deo?*"

Riley shrugged. She took the book from him and leafed through a few pages, but then, they heard voices outside the door. Van decided they'd pushed too far.

"We should get back to the party," he said. He took a few quick scans of the book and some more files he found interesting with his comm, then shut everything back in the safe. They let themselves out into the hallway, and Van took a detour to the bathroom so not to raise any more suspicions than he already had. Riley left to fend for herself out on the terrace.

Van stood around for a few minutes, staring at himself in the mirror. Somehow, a headache had sneaked up on him. He splashed a bit of cold water on his face, dried off with a towel and then left to find Riley and get them both out of there. Exiting the bathroom, though, he ran right into Charles Sinclair.

They stared at each other. Sinclair was in a white suit, no tie. His hair was short and wrapped in tight, greasy curls. His skin was tan, but that was typical in San Diego. He looked about 60, maybe older. Van wondered how quickly he could reach down and draw the gun he had strapped to his ankle. Instead, Sinclair smiled. Van reminded himself to breathe.

"You been in San Diego long, son?"

He considered the question carefully. "I did my residency, residencies here and I used to work in the ER up at Hillcrest General."

"You're a doctor. That's noble work. Healing people."

"Now I'm in research and development, downtown."

"Do you have a church home somewhere, Van?"

Right for the jugular. Van was so certain the guy was set to kill him that he'd not even considered being proselytized. One-track mind, these preachers. He shook his head.

"Well, then, maybe you give us a try some time. Maybe you'll find something you like. And stick with the Owens. They're good people." He winked again, headed down the stairs and returned to the party. Breathe, Van told himself.

A few moments later, he found Riley outside having an up-roarious conversation with a couple of twenty-something guys. Their smiles dimmed when Van stepped up and put his arm around her waist.

"Sweetie," she said. "There you are. Harry, Travis and Mark here were just telling me about their timeshare in Santa Barbara. They've invited us to spend a weekend. We really should go sometime."

"You, ah, you the boyfriend?" Harry asked, barely able to hide his disappointment. Van nodded.

"Hon, we should probably get going," he said.

She made a big show of checking her watch. "Yes, it is getting a little late. If you boys will excuse," she said, taking Van's arm and leading him across the patio.

"You enjoyed that a bit too much."

"A girl can dream."

"There were three of them. Which one were you dreaming about?"

"I have to pick just one?"

"Vixen."

"Troglodyte."

"I don't actually know what that is. Is that like a dinosaur?"

She laughed. Van told her about his one on one time with Charles Sinclair at the door to the bathroom. She agreed with his general assessment of the man's overall creepiness and the general ill feeling the whole lot of them — her phrase, not his — created. And the weapons? Maybe they could tip off the ATF, Riley suggested. But Van thought that might blow Station's cover, too. They said goodbye to Katie and Kyle, who enthusiastically insisted they stay longer because the "evening was still young." It took another 15 minutes to extract themselves from the party, but not before Van agreed to call them the next week about having dinner at Sabre, a $150 a head restaurant in La Jolla that the Owens couldn't say enough good things about.

A few minutes later, they were out of Point Loma and on

the freeway, heading home. That's when their comms started buzzing. Van pulled his from his pocket; a pulsating waveform flashed across his screen.

"What the hell does that mean?"

"Break in progress, it's close." She checked a map on her own comm and, within a few seconds, had the location pinned down to Fiesta Island, a small crop of land just off Mission Bay. Van massaged his forehead and let out a long sigh. He looked at Riley, though, and saw a gleam in her eye that frightened him a bit. Duty was calling.

"Okay," he said, and turned off the freeway so they could head back to Mission Bay. Riley called in to let Station know they were *en route*, and then flipped through all the readings on her comm.

"It's big," she said.

"Big as in…?"

"Big as in hurry."

As they got near, everything looked calm. Fiesta Island was popular with joggers and dog walkers, but it was just a flat, un-developed piece of land, ringed by a beach that enclosed a crop of wild grass and trees. There wasn't much to see, even in the daytime. When they got closer, though, Van realized there was anything to see at all, at least, anything *left* to see. The entire is-land — from the beach and the fire pits to the big field — was gone. In its place, a giant hole swirled, sucking in dirt from the mainland and water from the bay. Van pulled the car off onto the side of the road what he hoped was a safe distance away.

"Where did the island go?" he asked as they got out.

"Sometimes the breaks bring things here, sometimes they

take things away."

"Have you ever seen one take an entire island before?"

"No. No. This is new."

Van was about to say they should move farther back when the ground heaved underneath him, throwing them both into the air. Van came down with a thud on his backside, cracking his head off the crumbling pavement. Riley lay to his right on her back, trying to claw up the road as the ground broke apart. After a few false starts, Van got up to his knees and then back to his feet. He grabbed Riley and pulled them both to the side, narrowly avoiding the front bumper of his car as the break sucked it into oblivion. They ran for the freeway a few hundred feet away, but the ground gave out, dropping them into a newly formed hole were the 8 had once connected to Mission Bay Boulevard.

Then, as quickly as it had all started, the break sealed and the ground grew still. Van wanted nothing more than to rest, but water from the bay poured around them. He climbed his way up to solid ground, then reached down to help Riley.

"Damn," Van said, "I really liked that car."

Riley tried to stand, but her leg gave out and she fell. A slender piece of broken metal, probably a pipe fragment or — no, a part of street sign pole — stuck from her thigh. She called to Van, her voice quivering.

"What is it?"

"Don't panic." He twisted her leg enough so he could see the other side. The pole had gone straight through and was poking out the back. He usually carried a small trauma kit, but it was now wherever in the universe the car had ended up. He took off his sports coat and tore at the lining until he had enough material to wrap around the pole and keep it secured.

"What are you doing? Take it out Van, please."

"It may have hit your artery. I can't take it out, okay?"

She shook her head. Tears glistened in her eyes.

"You trust me?"

She starred at him, hard. Then she nodded. He stood and pulled his cell phone from his pocket to call for an ambulance, but he didn't have to. In the distance, he saw a spate of police cars, fire trucks and ambulances coming their way.

Cal and Ben met them at the hospital. The break had interrupted Cal's plan of spending the night asleep and Ben's plan of doing — well, he wouldn't say, but he was very unhappy about not being able to do it. They were both worried about Riley. Van tried to calm them.

"She's in surgery," he said. "It shouldn't take more than a half-hour, hour at the most. It missed the major artery they think, but… it's very close to the femoral nerve."

"What does that mean?" Ben asked.

"It's too early to tell."

"The U.S. Geological Survey is calling the break an earthquake for now, but it's not going to take them long to figure out that the shock wave patterns don't fit," Cal said.

"What about the press?"

"I've only caught glimpses of the reports, but they're just feeding the earthquake line back," Ben said.

Cal paced at the end of the room. "I'm not worried about the USGS. They'll hold the line on the earthquake story unless they can come up with some other plausible explanation. I'm guessing spacetime break won't be very high up on their list of possibilities. What's the collateral damage?"

"We have no way of knowing how many people were out there at the time," Van said. "We heard rumblings of a family reunion on the far side, but…"

Ben continued, "There's some flooding, obviously and I'm guessing that means the ground water tables in the area have shifted. I was on the phone with the Governor's office earlier and they've already asked the Army Corp. of Engineers to come in and assess the stability of the remaining land mass, considering that area, you know, holds up the base of Mt. Soledad and parts of La Jolla."

"What does this do to our numbers?" Cal asked.

Ben let out a long sigh. "This is really Riley's—"

"I'm asking you, Ben."

"This reset all our charts. It broke all the trend lines on the size and scope of the breaks. We weren't expecting anything like this for another year, at least."

"Van," Cal said. "Are you okay?"

"A few scrapes and bruises, but I'll heal."

"We'll pay for the car."

Van shrugged. "I've got insurance."

"How was the party?"

Van filled him on Kyle Owens' chest of weapons and his run in with the Reverend Charles Sinclair — the very same man who'd killed him two weeks ago. Cal listened to it all, then paced some more.

Riley was out of surgery and in recovery within the hour. Not long after that, she was settled into a private room and going on about how she needed to get back to Station One and update her models.

Van sat beside her bed. "Riley, the surgeon talked with you, right? You understand what he—"

"Yes, yes. He went on and on about it. The nerve is damaged, I know." She managed a smile. "Least it don't hurt, I can't feel much of anything down there right now."

They all looked to Van, as if he were supposed to pronounce her fine, give her a sterling prognosis. He too, managed a smile. "Some physical therapy and you'll be back at 100 percent in no time, I'm sure."

He was lying. The neurologist that examined her in the ER told Van she had a marked loss of proprioception and kinesthesia in the injured leg, big words to say she couldn't move or feel it very well. He took a quick glance at her chart to make sure the doctors had prescribed Neurontin, or maybe Topamax? She'd be glad they did. He was about to suggest they let her get some sleep when a news report about the island and the "earthquake" started playing on the television.

Riley made a "tsk" sound, and shook her head. "Everything in Southern California is a bloody earthquake. Damn fools. I should give them a call and set them straight." She reached for the bed-side phone, but Cal pulled it from her grasp.

"It's probably the morphine, or lingering effects from the anesthesia. Makes you a little loopy," Van said, trying to explain her behavior. "Riley, you look exhausted. Maybe you should get..."

The television caught Van's attention again, and his voice trailed off. The reporter on the scene cut to a taped interview he'd done a few minutes earlier, with a homeless woman named Delores. She was rotund, had wild grey hair and sun-weathered skin. She wore layers, about six that Van could see, and held a ratty-looking terrier in her arms. The graphic under her name said she lived in Mission Bay Park.

"I saw it as right as I'm standing in front of you now. It just swallowed the whole damn thing," she said, throwing her arms into the air. "The whole island. Torn it up in big, big pieces, like a blender." She spun her hand in a big spiral and made a whooshing sound to demonstrate. "It damn near took me with it. And Nixon, here." She looked down at her dog, then straight into the camera: "It weren't no earthquake."

"Son of a bitch," Cal said.

Cal dispatched Ben and Van to find Delores and make sure there was no repeat performance of her television news debut. But they searched the park and the beach until well into the morning with no luck. Finally, just before sunrise, they got a tip from a beat cop that she and Nixon sometimes slept on the steps of the convention center downtown, when the beach got too cold at night.

"She takes the trolley to Old Town then hops a bus with that dog in a paper bag come morning. Thinks we don't know it's in there," he said.

They thanked the cop and headed across town, but when they got to the convention center, a janitor told them Delores had already left. The same thing happened in Old Town. She'd been there, her dog in the bag, but she'd gone. By the time they'd made it back to Mission Bay, another news crew had found her first. This one was from Los Angeles. Van and Ben stood a distance away, listening and cringing as Delores told her story again: the sky ripping open, the vortex twisting and the island tearing apart. She finished, as she did the night before, with 'it weren't no earthquake.'

They approached her.

"You want an interview, too?" she asked, eyeing Van's sports coat and Ben's suit.

"No, actually. We were just... we were wondering if maybe..."

"We're here to explain what you saw last night," Ben said.

"Well?" Delores asked.

"Well... what you think you saw wasn't really what you... saw," Van said.

Delores cocked an eyebrow. "Come again?"

He looked to Ben for help, but got nothing. "Sometimes, the mind... when you're really tired. And you, see, something... extraordinary—"

Ben interrupted. "Would you consider not telling anyone else what you saw?"

"I've got another interview scheduled in just a few minutes. Live." She patted her hair, as though it were elaborately coiffed and not a wild ball of frizz.

"With whom?"

"CNN."

"Jesus Christ," Ben said.

"What would it take for you to not do that interview?"

"What you got?"

They looked at each other, then back to Delores. "A month in a hotel," Ben said.

"A year."

"No way."

"In the W."

"The W?"

"They take dogs."

"Six months," Van said. "In the W. That'll get you through the winter. But we have to go now. No more interviews."

She thought about it for a moment, then smiled. "That would be lovely, gentlemen. To which way is your car?" Ben pointed to their SUV, across the lot. Delores picked up Nixon and started that way. "My things," she said, indicating a pile of brimming Hefty bags stacked against a palm tree near the beach.

"I'll get them," Ben said.

Van started after Delores, but a woman's voice called out from behind him. He turned to see Councilwoman Zora coming toward him. He'd never met her in person, and had hoped he'd never have the occasion to do so. For fifty, though, Van had to admit she looked pretty good. She was in a white-knit, short-sleeved sweater with a scoop neck and trendy, striated jeans. Her hair had been cut since the election; in the last pictures Van had seen of her it was much longer.

"What can I do for you, Councilwoman?"

She flashed a bright smile, full of perfect teeth. "You recognize me?"

"It's not many candidates who can go on record disapproving of gay people, Jews, the poor, Hispanics — basically anyone not white or Republican — and still get elected in Southern California."

To her credit, she kept her smile locked in place. "I take it I didn't get your vote."

"When you won, I considered moving to Tijuana."

The smile vanished. "I was just wondering if you could tell me where you're taking that lovely lady over there? My chief of staff and I were hoping to speak with her." She looked back, behind her. A young man in a black suit was talking with the CNN crew across the lot. Van took him for her chief.

"Away from here," he said, "So she can have some privacy."

"I see. And you are…?"

"Her doctor. I'm… a doctor."

"That's very kind of you, Doctor. I don't think most would go to such lengths."

"Delores is special."

"Delores… I see. Is she ill?"

"What?"

"She seemed fine on television last night. I'm just wondering why she needs a doctor to come and rescue her?"

"I can't tell you that, of course."

"Of course." The smile returned. "Well, sorry I bothered you, Doctor. Have a wonderful day." She sauntered off, clearly feeling as though she'd just accomplished something. Van wasn't sure what, but he couldn't imagine it was anything good. He joined Ben at the car just as he finished loading Delores and her belongings.

"Who was that?" Ben asked, shutting the hatchback.

"Trouble."

Van woke just before noon, his head hurting. He must've cracked his head harder than he thought when the break tore apart Mission Bay. After they dropped Delores off at the hotel, they'd checked in on Riley, but she was still asleep and they'd left without waking her. Ben then decided that they, too, should get some sleep while they could, so he dropped Van off at his apartment downtown. It'd been a fitful, restless nap.

He crawled out of bed and stumbled into the bathroom. He flipped the lights and almost blinded himself, they seemed so bright. After taking a moment to adjust, he took a slow look in the mirror. There wasn't much to see on the front, but his back was one solid bruise from his shoulder blades to his tailbone. He took a quick shower, careful to clean all his new scrapes and cuts and then, satisfied nothing was bleeding, put on an undershirt and slipped into a pair of boxers. But before he could fix himself lunch, Cal called and said they needed him back at work. He groaned, went to his bedroom to retrieve his crumpled jeans and a new shirt and sports coat, and was off.

When he arrived at Station, Cal ushered him upstairs to the conference room. "We have some information on *Coram Deo*," he said.

"That was fast."

Ben was already there, as was another man, wearing a pair

of khakis and flowered shirt with one too many buttons undone, sitting across from him. The guy was short, bald, and except for the potbelly, unnervingly skinny. Van had never seen him before. Cal introduced him as Hunter Jackson, Station's historian.

"We have an historian?"

"We have pretty much everything," Ben said.

"I've had Walter searching for a reference to *Coram Deo* in our archives since you filed your report last night," Hunter said. "Of course, you know it's Latin and means 'for God.'"

They all looked at each other, then back at Hunter.

"Good," he said. "Well, I only came up with one reference, from a newspaper on Day Zero, in fact.

"Day Zero?" Van asked.

"The crash," Ben said.

Hunter pressed a few buttons on his console at the table, and an image of the newspaper clipping appeared, hovering in the air. "The report quotes a man named Cornelius Buckwald, the leader of a group of religious conservatives who were decrying reports of an alien space ship. They considered it an affront to God. The important part is here near the bottom. Buckwald identifies himself as a part of group that called themselves *Coram Deo*."

"And then?" Cal asked.

"And then nothing. The group, whatever its makeup was, vanished from recorded history. If they're active again, that's news to — well, everyone."

"Maybe they were never not active," Van said. "Maybe they went into hiding."

"So, what? They're now out and proud and trying to kill us?" Cal asked.

"We protect the thing they hate."

"The power of religious fervor," Ben said. "Seems like there's got to be more to it than that." Simultaneously, Ben and Hunter looked to Cal. He sat silently, staring back at them. The whole scene caught Van off guard. Clearly, they knew something that he didn't know, and it seemed to be that Cal knew something they all didn't know. Finally, Hunter spoke up.

"I wasn't able to search the squad leader's journals. If they've been active recently, maybe Wright made some note of it. If you grant me access—"

"No." Cal said. "I'll check them. If there's anything in there we need to know, I'll fill you all in. That's it for now." He pushed back from the table and left the room. Hunter looked at them and smiled, meekly, before gathering up his files and leaving too.

"What was that about?" Van asked.

"Former squad leader's journals are only accessible by the current squad leader," Ben said.

"So Wright, he was—"

"She. Wright was Cal's predecessor."

"Cal keeps a lot of secrets, doesn't he?"

Ben looked at Van like he'd just said something stupid. "Cal is the secret," he said.

"I don't understand."

"No one else does, either. Welcome to Station One."

Fiesta Island was just the beginning. The next day, an entire apartment building went missing in North Park, along with eighty-five of its residents. And then, a break near a school talent show in La Jolla froze an eighth grade dance troupe in the middle of a *Single Ladies* rendition for more than an hour. The parents were hysterical, so Cal sealed them all in and gassed the auditorium with a sedative until the break subsided. They told everyone afterward that it was carbon monoxide poisoning. Another break hit a movie theater a few days later, on a Friday night. Time stopped for days and they had to call the National Guard to contain the area.

It went on that way for weeks. Van was so busy dealing with the singularity's wake that finding time to seal the containment unit was difficult. He started coming in early in the morning, before the sun was up, and staying late at night. He worked non-stop, tearing through test after test after test, constantly refining the procedures and steps. At one point, he was on such a roll that he went four days without ever even going home. He would've missed Thanksgiving entirely, had Riley not come in and brought him some turkey.

"Look at you," Van said. With the help of a cane, she was walking. She set the plate of food on his desk and took a seat.

"Therapy is going on all right."

"No more wheel chair?"

"No more wheel chair. And thank god."

"How's the pain? Do you need me to prescribe something?"

"It's not too bad, actually. I am going a little stir crazy at home, though."

"December will be here in no time."

"I know, I know. I need recovery time. You've made that

abundantly clear. But I'm doing so well."

"All the more reason not to push things."

She looked down at her leg, which she'd propped up on the edge of his desk. "The doctors, they avoid my questions."

Van pushed aside the stack of files he'd been trying to organize. "What kind of questions?"

"The damage to the nerve, it's mostly permanent, is it not? It won't be getting much better, will it?"

He shook his head.

"I'm not going to be much use in the field, hobbling along on a crutch."

"I haven't known you very long, but I can't imagine this keeping you down."

She smiled, meekly, but Van was still glad to see it. "I have something to show you," he said.

He led her down to the lab, a sprawling, sterling white room filled with work stations along the walls and a long table in the center. A trough filled with water lay on it, at the far end. Van cautioned her not to touch it.

She looked over the edge. "Is that what I think it is?"

A small square floated in the trough, moored by jets of water. It looked like a piece of glass until Van asked Walter to alternate the current, and it turned opaque white.

"It's stable. We're still gathering data on the structure, but based on our tests, it's an atom-for-atom replication of the containment unit's walls."

"How did you do it?"

"I was in sickbay self-treating my latest concussion — courtesy of a spacetime break yesterday that, once again, knocked me on my ass — and I was thinking about how our brains are really just conduits for electrical activity. I knew we were missing some essential component... it just never occurred to me before what that was."

"So you—"

"Juiced it, with about 20,000 volts. Give or take an electron."

"You brought it to life." She gleamed.

"Well, maybe. In the strictest biological, non-Frankenstein way."

"So now what?"

He sighed. "Now we have a new problem. We needed to replicate this stuff to test my treatments, right? And to test my treatments we need to duplicate the fracture in the containment unit. But the fibers in this stuff actually interlock in response to stress. It's like the more we hit it, the stronger it gets."

"It's indestructible?"

Van nodded. "And unfortunately... a time-wasting dead end."

5

It was early in the morning, a few days before Christmas, when the alarm on Van's comm blared. He was already awake, though, hunched over the toilet. Pills, ice packs, massages — none of it seemed to stem his raging headaches. They started slow, got worse at night, nothing unusual about that, he reasoned. Stress, tension. This morning, though, he woke with a pain above his eyes so excruciating he couldn't see straight. After spending an hour on the bathroom floor, he called Riley to make sure she and Ben could handle the break on their own and then put in a call to Dr. Richard Bower, an internist he'd done a rotation with as a resident.

Bower was gruff, had no bedside manner and should've retired about fifteen years ago. Van loved him. He cleared a space for Van in his clinic schedule that morning and after blowing Cal off with an excuse about the flu, made the trek across town for his appointment.

It went about as he expected.

"We should get you in the OR as soon as possible after the holiday," Dr. Bower said, his eyes glued to a set of MRI scans of Van's head. "You know we can't wait on this."

Indeed.

Van stood, staring at the ocean through his apartment windows. It was unseasonably warm, even for San Diego, but he decided to stay inside anyway. This was the first Christmas he hadn't put up his tree or hung a stocking. Mostly, he hadn't the time. Since Thanksgiving, the longest they'd gone without seeing a break was three days, right at the beginning of the month. If he wasn't in the field with Ben or Riley, he was back at Station running experiments on the containment material they'd replicated. Nearly a month after he'd created it — twenty-two days, three hours, four minutes and ten seconds, to be exact — and he was only beginning to understand its composition. Riley told him not to blame himself. It wasn't his fault they couldn't recreate the fracture, she said. He did blame himself, though. He'd led them down this path, and, at best, it was all academic.

About three that evening, another break hacked apart spacetime somewhere out over the ocean. Van was barely literate when it came to reading the waveforms and data streams his comm splashed on screen during each event, but he'd learned enough to know it was big. Riley called a few minutes later, and she confirmed what he'd thought: the break was large and it was a few miles off the coast. But, she also told him some surfers stumbled across something washed up on the beach not long after. Something big, from the sound of it.

"A whale?" Van asked.

"I don't think they'd be calling us if it were a whale, Van."

"Okay. What beach?"

"Black's Beach? In Torrey Pines?"

Of course. Fitting. "You ever been to Black's?"

"Nope."

"Well, it's a little remote. And... it's also clothing optional."

Silence, then: "What? No. Well, this'll be interesting." Van could almost hear the smile in her voice.

But when they were finally all the way up to Torrey Pines and standing on the cliffs, looking at the craggy trail meandering down to the beach below — far below — her enthusiasm waned.

"You've got to be kidding me," she said.

"I told you it was a bit of a hike," Van said.

"You didn't tell me I'd need a mountain goat. This is ridiculous. There has to be another way down."

Van shook his head. They could go back to La Jolla Shores, but it'd be a good three to four mile trek, and the tide was in, so part of it would be underwater. The same from the north. They could've gone to the Embarcadero and got the boat, but it wasn't like they could just drive it up on the beach.

"Riley, this is a tough hike, even for people with full of use of both legs. Maybe I should go on alone—"

"Absolutely not. I won't hear of it."

"But, coming back—"

She turned to face him. "Do you see this face? It is resolved, is it not?"

"It is."

"Then let's go. I'll need just a bit help, but I can do it."

"You don't have anything to prove to me, or to anyone else."

"Yes, I do."

He put his arm out so she could take hold, and they started down the path.

"But, if I fall off this cliff and die I am so coming back and haunting this place. And you."

"Check. Haunting, got it."

"We really have to talk with Cal about getting a helicopter."

"I hear they're hard on gas."

"Perhaps they make a hybrid?"

They made it to the bottom of the trail in just under thirty minutes, a good clip even with Riley's bad leg. It ended at a small crag that stood about seven or eight feet above the beach, so they had to jump to the sand below. Riley slipped, though, and landed on her face. She stood slowly, dusted the sand from her suit and hurled a string of swear words that made Van blush.

"If this is all for some beached whale, I'm going—"

She stopped, distracted by a sinewy, naked man ambling down the beach in front of them.

"That make it all worth it?" Van asked.

She nodded. "Certainly helps."

"I thought you said they wouldn't call us for a whale?"

"Shut up Van."

They started on their way, Riley leading with a rough set of coordinates. After a few minutes of walking, a white lifeguard truck pulled up beside them. A man, lean, toned and wearing nothing but a pair of little red shorts and a dark, even tan, sat in the driver's seat.

"You guys here for the... the problem?"

Van and Riley glanced at each other, and then Van nodded. They slid into the passenger's side of the truck, and the man introduced himself as Sgt. Bobby Palmer, chief of Tower 24.

"Some surfers stumbled across it, called us," he said.

"And no one has any idea what it is?" Riley asked.

"No, they have ideas," Palmer said. "Just none that make any sense."

After a short trip up the beach, they stopped just ahead of an outcrop that extended from the cliffs and a ways into the water. They got out of the truck and followed Palmer around the edge of the cliff and through a path up the rocks. From there, they had a clear view of why they'd been called: a small crowd of surfers and a few naked beach-goers had gathered, gawking at a motionless beast spread out across the sand. It was white and sheeny, had a long neck and an even longer tail, an arrow shaped head with round, silvery-blue eyes on the sides and two wings the flowed from its back like sail cloth flapping in the wind.

"So, am I wrong," Van said, looking at Riley, "or is that a dragon?"

They told Palmer to pull the crowd back and cordon off the beach from both ends. He'd become suspiciously quiet since Van had dropped 'dragon' and did as he was told without question.

Riley and Van climbed down the rocks and marched heedfully toward it, watching for any signs of life. They stopped, still more than thirty feet away.

"You ever seen anything like this?"

Riley shook her head. "It's so, so big."

"It looks dead," Van said.

He was guessing, but he didn't see any movement in its torso, which meant it probably wasn't breathing — if it needed to breath. Its eyes, the size of frisbees, were still; its pupils steady and lifeless. He pulled out his comm to scan for electrical activity in its nervous system, but the phase distortions interfered with his sensors.

"One of us will have to get closer," he said.

"Don't look at me, I've got just one good leg."

"You just hiked down a three-hundred foot cliff."

"But you're the doctor."

Its head, from neck to nose, was at least ten feet. He imagined the size of its teeth and then promptly scolded himself for imaging such things. He caught a glimpse of one of its talons, sticking out from under its torso. It was easily the size of his forearm.

But there was no other way to do this. He took a deep breath, moved in close and scanned it again. Nothing. No brain activity that he could detect. He adjusted the settings on his comm to detect a wider base of vital signs, but still got nothing.

"It's really dead," he said, calling back to Riley.

The dragon's skin — a mosaic of irregularly shaped scales — radiated an array of mesmerizing colors, like oil skimming water. He took a few steps closer, close enough so he could reach out and put his hand on it; it was still warm. The skin was tender.

Riley stepped up beside him, her eyes locked on the dragon's head.

"What are we going to do with it?"

"I don't know."

"We've never had an incursion this large."

Van filed that away to think about later. It could just be an outlier. The thing didn't survive the transition anyway. For now, he just had to worry about its size. He could worry about what its size meant, later.

"We close the beach until the sun is down, then… airlift it back to Station so we can do some tests, imaging and stuff there and then, I don't know… dispose of it somehow."

"You're not thinking of flying this thing across the city?"

"We can't exactly leave it on the beach."

She crossed her arms and cocked her head slightly. It was the stance Van had seen at the top of the cliff, her resolved stance.

"If you've got a better idea, I'm listening," he said.

She started to speak, but her comm flashed red and its alarm boomed, cutting her off. Van's went off a second later. Riley glanced through the readings.

"I can't locate the event horizon," she said. "I think, I think we're in the middle of it." She looked up at him, panicked.

Then the sky split open. The force of it lifted Van from his feet and sent him soaring across the beach. He tumbled head over heels into the sand, but when he looked back, he saw himself still standing near the dead dragon, at least 60 feet away. Then he was in the air again, and then, he hit the sand again. He lost track of Riley. She was beside him through it all, but not. It was loud, then totally silent. He sat up, finally grounded — he thought, at least — to one place. Riley was beside him, wiping dirt out of her eyes and spitting up sand.

"What the fuck was that?" he asked.

"Van—" she pointed behind him.

The sky was on fire. Van pulled himself to his feet, gritting his teeth as a torrent of pain ripped through his legs and arms. He looked up in time to see another dragon spill out of the break. It tumbled head over tail, falling toward the earth. Van held his breath, praying that it was dead like the first one. But then, it flapped its wings and let out a screech so thunderous the ground trembled. Yeah, very much alive. Van grabbed Riley and dove to the ground just as the it swooped over them. It banked toward the sky and after circling for a few moments, perched itself on the cliffs.

"We have to do something," Van said. He looked back. The crowd of onlookers had taken cover in the rocks, but that wouldn't do them much good. "We should get these people out of here."

"If that means getting us out of here, then I'm all for it," she said.

They backed away, taking small, slow steps so as to not startle it.

"It looks smaller than the other one," Riley said.

She was right. It was maybe a third of the size of the dead dragon on the beach. A baby? Not that it mattered.

"Maybe whatever defensive abilities it has aren't fully developed. Maybe—"

It screeched again, unleashing a harrowing siren that shook

Van from the inside out.

"I don't think so," Van said.

The dragon looked down at them like a dog who'd just spotted a squirrel. Then, it opened its mouth and a fiery burst of light spewed out, tearing at them like a missile.

Van heard nothing, felt nothing, saw nothing. When he came to, Riley was standing over him, yelling. That's what he assumed, anyway. All he could hear was a high-pitched ringing and the sound of his heart beating in his ears. The air was thick with dust and sand and the smell of burnt rocks. He looked back. The outcropping, where all those people had taken cover, was gone, leaving a house-sized crater in its place.

Riley shook him. What the hell did she want? He was sure shaking him wasn't the way to get it. He looked up at her. She was definitely screaming. He was almost glad he couldn't hear. A shadow passed over them. The dragon was still there, and it was circling.

He heard the muffled sound of his name. It was Riley. She said it again and he heard it louder this time, clearer. "Van!" He got it that time. She was still screaming. "Van! Answer me!"

"Yeah, yes."

"Oh my god, are you all right?"

He wasn't sure.

"I'm okay," he said, nodding.

He sat up, slowly, grimacing at the pain in his back and arms. The sky was so bright. Palmer was a few feet away — at least, a few recognizable parts of him were. A couple of the surfers appeared to be alive, but most of them weren't. Riley helped him to his feet, but he struggled to get his bearings.

"We have to take it down," she said.

The thought had occurred to him. But a .22 wasn't going to cut it. Riley pulled out her comm and relayed the situation back to Station. They needed something big. Anyone who suggested a tank wouldn't have been crazy. Van watched as the dragon stopped circling and settled back down on a ledge far above. It was too heavy, apparently, because the cliff crumbled, and the dragon fell about fifty feet before getting a grip on the rocks. It hung there, its head craned toward them and its eyes locked on their every move.

It's scared, Van thought. Feeling was mutual.

"Cal's activating a tactical unit," Riley said. "We should take cover until they get here."

"If we move, it'll kill us."

"Okay, then, I'm open to suggestions."

But Van didn't have any. There was nothing they could do. Nowhere they could run. Maybe, if they didn't startle it, the dragon would just hang there until the tactical unit arrived. That theory held for about all of ten seconds, when it launched itself from the cliff side and swooped toward them. They couldn't out run it. There wasn't anywhere to go even if they could. It screeched its horrible screech and swooped so close to their heads that its wake sent Van and Riley spiraling to the ground.

But it didn't fire bomb them. It didn't even try to eat them. Instead, it pulled up and flew higher and higher into the sky until they couldn't see it any longer.

Just like that, it was gone.

By the time Cal arrived on the beach, the damage had been done.

Five people were dead, including Palmer. Six more were hurt. A mix of blunt force injuries and burns, as far as Van could tell. The survivors were being airlifted to Hillcrest, but he didn't think they'd be survivors for very long. One or two might have a chance, but not a very good one. The tactical unit had been diverted to an unpopulated area just northeast of the city, going off eyewitness calls to 911 of a very large bird. The last they'd heard, they'd caught up with it just south of Julian. That was fifteen minutes ago.

Cal paced. He tried to raise the tactical team on his comm again, to no avail. He turned to Van.

"Can you bring this thing down?"

Van's eyes grew big. "With what, my startling good looks?"

"We need something Van."

"Our tactical unit couldn't stop it and they have missile launchers. What do you expect me to do?"

"It has to have a weakness."

Van stewed. Cal and Riley both looked at him. He started to shake his head, but then turned back to the dead dragon still on the beach behind them. The tide was coming in, and the water lapped up around it with each wave.

"What are you thinking?" Cal asked.

Van shook his head. He was going out on a big old limb. "Its skin is soft. A tranquilizer dart might penetrate it, but... there's no guarantee we have a tranquilizer that will work. And again, I want to point out the whole missile launchers couldn't stop it thing."

Cal nodded. "Best plan we've got. Sounds good to me." He

turned to Riley. "Can you track it?"

She crossed her arms and thought for a few seconds. "It's leaving a temporal trail. Disrupting spacetime in a way that we can follow, so yeah, I… well, I think so."

Cal smiled, the way he always did when he was irrationally confident their hackneyed plans would succeed. Van wished he could dispel reality with the same finesse. He was about to say something, when all three of their comms flashed warnings and sounded alarms. Another break.

"Where is it?" Cal said.

"A better question is 'how big?'," Van said.

Riley flipped furiously through her readings, but just shook her head. "I don't know."

Van braced for the worst. The last time a break erupted near them he'd nearly been split into infinite versions of himself. Traversing the entire timeline of existence in a single instant wasn't something he'd enjoyed. But then, the alarms dimmed and there was no massive explosion, no bending of quantum physics, no massive explosion of temporal energy. The ground rumbled a bit, but that was all. Riley turned toward the ocean, scanning with her comm.

"I'm getting a lock. It's fuzzy, but it looks like the epicenter was a mile or so away, near the floor of the San Lucas chasm. I can't tell if anything made it through, but it was a big break, bigger than the two that unleashed our dragons."

Cal and Riley stood discussing whatever readings she could get, which, as it turns out, weren't many. It was so large the phase distortions were clouding the comm's sensors. They'd get a better idea once they were back at Station and could pull down data from the satellites, Riley said. Van, though, was distracted by the water. The tide was receding far too rapidly. He'd never seen anything like it. Something was swallowing up the ocean, pulling it away and dramatically expanding the beach. A few moments ago, the water was on their heels. Now it was twenty feet out. Then fifty. Van swallowed hard. He turned back to Riley and Cal.

"Run," he said.

They fell silent, staring at him.

"Run!"

They grabbed Riley by the arms and sprinted for the cliffs, hitting the base at full speed. They threw themselves up, climbing as hard and as fast as they could. Van looked back, only to see a wall of water rising behind them, heading for the San Diego coast.

The tsunami cracked against the cliffs, sending a shock wave through the rocks that bounced Van into the air. He flailed wildly, slapping his arms at anything that jutted far enough out that he could get a hand hold. He grabbed a precipice at the last second, dangling just a few feet above the raging water. He clung to the rocks with one arm, struggling to hold his grip and watching as the ocean swallowed the coastline. Just when he thought he couldn't hold on any longer, Cal managed to grab his wrist and pull him to a ledge.

They spent the next hour climbing. Riley struggled, having just one good leg, but she managed along with Van and Cal's help.

Van, though, was soaked from the spray of the waves and had nothing to shield himself from the wind. The sun had set, and the temperature had dropped. By the time they reached a crevice near the top that they could walk through, he was exhausted and shivering and could barely walk. He clawed his way up the last few feet and collapsed in the dirt. Riley and Cal followed. The three of them lay on the ground, gasping for breath. Finally, Riley spoke.

"How bad do you think it is?"

No one answered. The break must've swallowed a part of the ocean floor, Van reasoned. It was such a quick, massive displacement of land that it sent a wall of water hurtling toward the coast. He thought about the beach communities, about Mission Valley. They wouldn't have had any warning.

Cal pushed himself up to a sitting position. "You two able to move?" he asked.

They both pushed themselves up, nodding.

"Go. Get the dragon."

"What are you going do?" Riley said.

"I'll make my way back to Station. One of us should be there."

"They're going to want to know what happened," Van said.

Cal didn't answer. He pushed himself to his feet, and walked off into the darkness. Riley and Van did the same.

Riley had fixed the position of the dragon somewhere in the deserts east of Los Angeles, moving in a haphazard pattern into the wilderness, but for a while, Van wasn't sure they'd even get out of the city, let alone to the desert. The beach communities were under water, as was most of Mission Valley and the number 8 freeway. News was spotty, but a radio report put the dead at 150,000 and rising.

"How's the leg?" Van asked, as they were driving.

"It's been better. I lost my cane when we started climbing."

"We're not far from Barstow, we can stop and get a new one."

She shook her head. "No time. It looks like our dragon is finally slowing down."

"Where?" Van asked.

"Las Vegas."

It must've been the bright, shiny lights, Riley said.

"You're, scared, confused, flying for hours in the dark and then you spot a glowing beacon in the middle of the desert. Where would you stop?"

"In-N-Out Burger, if I had my choice. I'm starving."

She rolled her eyes and diverted her attention back to a phone call. Their long-shot plan was to get the city manager to shut down the city's power, no small feat considering it took them ten minutes just to get the watch commander on the phone. From what Van heard, he was with her until she said the words "dragon attack."

"He hang up?"

"Not before calling me a few names."

Van parked the car just off the strip on Harman Avenue, and after pulling a dart rifle and box of tranquilizers they had picked up at Station One out of the trunk, helped Riley walk the few blocks to the Strip.

"Okay," he asked. "Where do we go?"

"It's not a GPS. I've got a radius around the phase distortions it's causing, but that's it."

"How big of a radius?"

She hesitated. "Five... miles. Maybe 15."

"Miles? That's fantastic. How are we going to find this thing?"

Behind him, a dull roar exploded into a burst of twisting metal and explosions. He turned in time to see the dragon smash-land into the side of one of the casinos, its claws tearing into the facade of the building. It unleashed a fireball that tore through rows of cars on the strip, flipping buses and trucks and people into the air in a torrent of fire and debris.

"Oh. There it is."

6

As carnage went, the dragon was a connoisseur. Tourists ran and screamed and died as smoldering debris piled up on the streets.

"I bet the city manager will take our call now," Van said.

The dragon perched itself on top of the Eiffel Tower and, for the moment, seemed content to sit there and not kill anyone. Van pointed to the pedestrian bridge that crossed the strip just below Harman Avenue. They crossed the street and climbed the stairs, then walked out to the center, careful to keep watch of the dragon. Van set to work loading the rifle. He pulled a dart with a needle the size of a railroad spike from the case he'd grabbed from the car.

"I'm flashing back to your speech about the tactical team," Riley said.

"Cal said the survivors reported not even getting a shot off. Don't worry. I'm not worried."

"You're not?"

Van looked at her. "I've got three darts. This stuff can drop an elephant, so dragon should be… no problem."

As he took aim, the dragon shifted around on the tip of the tower so its head pointed his way. Sirens sounded in the distance, which meant local emergency crews were on their way. The National Guard would probably follow. More people to burn.

Van fired. The dart hit the dragon in the neck, just under its snout. It cocked its head and looked at him like he'd pelted it with a rock. Van bent down to reload, but Riley yanked him to his feet as the dragon spewed a swath of fire their direction. They ran as the bridge disintegrated under their feet.

At Station, Cal tried to assess the status of the alien ship, but half his staff was unaccounted for, and half of the ones he knew were still alive hadn't made it in. The others weren't functioning well.

Carlos paced the entire length of the second level and his chief lab assistant was in a corner, sobbing. The entire accounting department was loading staplers and adding machines into boxes for some reason, and Claire, a computer tech, was sitting on the operations deck with a potted plant from her office. "There's water pouring into the parking garage," someone shouted from the stairs. "We've just received a report that a pylon under the 805 has collapsed," another said.

Cal called everyone to a halt and told them to calm down, focus and do their jobs.

"Priority one," he said, "is to get a team out to the landing to check the condition of the ship first hand. Priority two is monitoring Van and Riley's progress and help them as we can. Our third priority is to provide logistical support for the search and rescue efforts in the city. Then, after that's done, I want someone to tell me why the fuck this is all happening."

Van checked himself: all his arms and legs were still attached. The scent of charred flesh tinged the air, and he thought he heard someone crying. He was on the ground, but how'd he get there? Oh, yeah. The dragon. Riley? He rolled his head from side to side, but didn't see her. He'd have to get up. He hated that idea, but saw no alternative. He pushed himself to his feet, then scanned the area. The world had caved in around him. The bridge was gone, or at least, appeared to be gone. He wasn't actually sure where he was at that particular moment. Concrete. There was hard concrete, and yellow paint. He was on a road. The remains of a car burned to his left. Yeah, definitely on a road. He looked up. The turrets that held the bridge were still standing, yet charred. He'd fallen.

Slowly, he tested each limb. They hurt like hell, but it didn't seem like anything was broken. Then, he heard Riley's voice. She hobbled down a set of stairs that were once attached to the bridge, then climbed over the rubble to him.

"God, I thought I'd lost you. You fell. Are you okay?" Van nodded. His head felt like it weighed a thousand pounds, but generally, yes, he was okay. Riley looked around him. "Where's the rifle?" she asked.

Van looked around, then shook his head. "Doesn't matter. I lost our last two cartridges." He looked across the street. The dragon was on the ground, nosing through a pile of cars.

"What do we do now?"

"I don't know."

He pulled out his comm and raised Station. Carlos answered.

"What's up? You guys dragon hunting?"

"Where's Cal?"

"Things are a bit chaotic right now, little buddy."

"We could use some help here, Carlos."

"Not going well?"

The dragon roared, belching out a fireball that burned a hole in the road.

"You could say that. Ideas, please?"

"You shot it up with the darts?"

"One of them. It didn't work. The others are gone."

"What other weapons we got?"

"I've got guns and rocks, Carlos."

"Okay... oh! Sound?"

"We can hear you."

"No, I mean, sound. Infrasound. Remember, I told you about this?"

He sounded so excited, so pleased with himself. Van had no idea what he was talking about. "You did?"

"Not long after you started, I was at the DOD symposium in D.C., where the Navy cardiologist presented research on the effects of infrasound on the body? He thought it could be weaponized. I sent you an email, asked for your insight, which you never responded to, no biggie, whatever. Then I gave a twenty minute presentation on it at the weekly briefing…"

"Sorry."

"You guys never listen to me."

"Carlos!"

"Okay. Too much low frequency sound affects the organs, the heart especially, disrupts beating, slows it down."

"How do we generate infrasound?"

"You can't. At least not artificially. I mean if you had the right equipment, and a controlled lab environment, you could do some really amazing things with—"

"Carlos, focus."

"The tsunami. Tsunamis, earthquakes, all kinds of severe natural phenomena produce subsonic sounds, that's why animals freak out right before they happen. They can hear it but we can't."

"So what good does that do us?"

"The surveillance apps in your comms, they're like dash cams in police cruisers, right? So they would've been recording when it happened."

Van looked at Riley. "Surveillance apps?"

"Didn't Cal tell you?" Carlos asked.

"No."

Silence. "Well, I'm sure he meant to."

"Right. Do you have access to the audio?"

"Yeah, it'll take me a bit to isolate a wave form at the right frequency. I'll feed it back to you. But, you're going to need to a strong source, like a really, really strong source."

The dragon had taken to the air again. It circled like a vulture, then settled across the street, atop what was left of the facade of one of the casinos. Up the road, where the Strip intersected with Tropicana Avenue, a line of police cars had formed. Van thought he could make out the lines of a tank.

"This is Vegas. What about a night club, a sound system, will that work?"

"Maybe," Carlos said. "If you can get it positioned directly under the speakers."

Riley consulted a map on her comm, then pointed to the building sitting down the road, on the street corner. Its side wall was gone, exposing a large dance floor to the outside.

"Go," Van said to Riley. "And I'll bring you a dragon."

"Van—"

"I'll distract it. Go."

Van took off before should could say anything else. He dove behind an overturned police cruiser and rummaged around until he found an emergency kit in the wreckage. He pulled a few road flares from the bag and then, bonus, found a flare gun with a full array of cartridges. He ripped them out, loaded the gun, and walked down the center of Las Vegas Boulevard. The dragon was perched high atop a casino, curled into a ball. It watched him.

Van yelled up at it and waved his arms in the air, but it didn't stir. He glanced back. He couldn't see Riley, which hopefully meant she'd made it inside the club and was hard at work patching her comm into their sound system. He took a deep breath, steeled himself for what he was about to do, and then fired the gun.

The flare knocked the dragon square in the head, surprising it more than anything. It craned its neck to look down at Van,

obviously confused as to why a tiny little bug had thrown something hot and bright at it. It pushed up onto its legs, then dropped
the hundred or so feet to the sidewalk below, shaking the ground
as it landed. It sat there, studying him.

Van had hoped for more of a reaction, but at least he had its
rapt attention. He took one of the road flares from his pocket and
pulled the striking tab. The dragon trained on the bright light,
swaying back and forth to match the motion of Van's arm as he
waved it in the air.

"Good dragon. Good, good dragon," he said.

Cal stood on the operations deck, turning from computer screen
to computer screen, taking it all in.

"Walter, can you access the FEMA mainframe from here?"

"Yes, Cal."

"Get me a list of authorized emergency actions for the tsunami event. I want to know what their plans are."

A list of documents popped up on the screen in front of him.
He was halfway through them when Ben stepped off the elevator,
soaking wet.

"You know the parking garage is flooded?"

"So I've heard."

"What the hell is going on?"

"Singularity ripped a hole in the sea bed."

"The ship?"

"I've got a team on the way out there now."

"It's chaos outside. I wasn't sure I was even gonna make it down here, and what is Claire doing to that plant?"

"She's calmed down a lot."

Walter called for Cal's attention, telling him he had an incoming call on a secure line in the conference room. "Who is it?"

"The president, Cal."

He looked at Ben, then left for the conference room. Ben called after him: "Where are Riley and Van?"

The dragon focused on the road flare in Van's hand.

Its eyes flickered and its nostrils flared. It flapped and then folded its wings. Alive, up close, Van saw it differently than the dead one on the beach. It was an animal, and it was scared. Another time, another place and a lot less dead people lying around, he might have felt sorry for it.

He turned and ran toward the club, the flare out to his side and the dragon trailing uncomfortably close behind. He bounded across the sidewalk, navigating a path around smoldering cars and bodies, then over a pile of rubble that was once the front wall of the club. He slipped when he hit the dance floor, dropping the flare and sending it skidding across the room. Riley banged on the glass windows of the sound booth to get his attention.

"I've got it! Now get out of here!" she said.

She shambled for the exit on the other side of the room. Van clamored to his feet and tried to follow, just as the dragon tried to force its way inside the building. It was too big to fit though the hole in the wall, and its spastic squirming made the whole place shake. Van tripped as the building's foundation rumbled. He tried to orient himself, but it was too late. The dragon burst into the room. It stalked close, its head low, eyes locked on Van. He was trapped against the back wall. The dragon's sulfurous breath wafting over him. There were no lights, just the red glow of the flare lying to his left.

They held like that, for what seemed an eternity. The seconds ticked off in Van's brain, but haphazardly, like something was screwing with his clock. It made him dizzy. Finally, as slowly and as carefully as he could, he pulled himself up to his feet. The dragon bellowed, enveloping him in a deafening wall of sound.

Van backed up a few steps to the door. Just as he found the latch, the dragon charged and Van thrust himself backward, bursting out onto the ground behind the club, where Riley had been waiting.

"What the hell happened in there?"

The dragon hit the wall, but only half its head made it through the door. The wall cracked and buckled as it writhed inside the frame, trying to break open a hole big enough that it could escape. It pulled back inside suddenly, and Van figured it was either about to take another, final run or blast the place open with fire. Neither scenario was ideal. He turned to Riley.

"Do it."

She hit a button on her comm. Van didn't hear anything and was worried that it hadn't worked. But then, he felt an odd tickling sensation move up through his feet and into his chest. Through the door, he saw the dragon thrash wildly. Riley took Van by the arm and pulled him away. The building shuddered and rumbled, and the dragon screamed.

"Turn it up," Van said.

Riley hit a few more buttons on her comm and the building's shaking turned into a bounce. It broke away from its frame before collapsing in on itself.

As the dust settled, there was no more movement, no more sound, no more screaming dragon.

With Cal's help, Van and Riley arranged for a trailer truck to haul the dragon back to San Diego, so it could be put in stasis in one of their holding bays. He injected it with as much tranquilizer as they could wrestle away from the vets who oversaw the animal exhibits at one of the casinos, and then sent it ahead.

Van and Riley arrived back at Station One themselves early that morning. As day had broke, the tsunami's wrath became clear: Coronado Island, the beach communities and Silver Strand were just gone. The water was receding from Mission Valley, but slowly. The 805 and 15 freeways were bearing the brunt of overflow traffic from the 8, which was mostly underwater. Officials pleaded with people to stay home, but from what Van had seen on their way into town, not many listened.

Riley locked herself in her office the minute they got back, probably going over the sensor data they had on the last break. Van glanced up from the control deck every once in a while, and if she wasn't staring at her computer screens, she was on the phone. A few other analysts went in and out, carrying stacks of papers and files. Cal mostly paced in between calls from people who, if Van was correctly interpreting the bits and pieces he'd been hearing, placed the blame for everything that had happened in the last twenty-four hours on him and Station One.

"Merry Christmas," Ben said. He rolled a chair over next to Van and sat down, then handed him a small box wrapped in silver paper and a green ribbon. Van hadn't been expecting a gift. "I'd planned to give it to you yesterday, but you know. Dragon attack, tsunami, the fabric of time and space unraveling."

"I don't have anything for you."

Ben shook his head. "I just like giving gifts." He stood, patted Van on the shoulder and then left him with his present. Inside, he found a silver pocket watch, the kind with a hinged case that protects the face and crystal. He ran his thumb over the casing; it was elaborately engraved in a strange, annular pattern. On the inside, two red hands sat atop an exposed network of shiny gears. However old the watch was, they'd not lost their brilliance. There was a card in the box that read: "Every good Jules Verne fan should have one."

Van carefully slid the watch into his jacket pocket. He started on his way to find Ben and thank him, but was interrupted when Riley burst from her office and asked for Cal. He'd never seen the look she had on her face, a mix of abject terror and exhaustion. Van pointed down the walkway, to Cal's office. She turned and went off without a word. A second later, Ben stepped up behind him.

"What do you suppose that's about?"

"Good news, I'm sure." They stood silent, for just a moment. "Thank you," Van said. "That was... I feel like I can't accept it, it's too much."

Ben shrugged. "Sure you can."

"How did you know I liked Jules Verne? From watching me all those months? I do have a worn copy *20,000 Leagues Under the Sea* that I read like twenty times a year."

He shook his head. "The day the blob exploded and we were talking in the shower. You quoted him, 'What goes on in those distant depths' — remember?"

Ben smiled and left him standing alone by the railing on the second level. Van hadn't realized he'd recognized the quote. Maybe there were quite a few things he hadn't realized about Ben. Just then, Cal and Riley emerged from Cal's office and called for them to all go to the conference room. Once inside, Cal locked the doors and flipped a switch that sealed the room's windows from the outside. They settled into their seats, and a few seconds later, the screen hanging at the far end of the conference table came to life with an image of the presidential seal. Then, President Howe appeared.

No one else seemed to be as startled by this as Van was. He hadn't even voted for her.

"Have you figured out what the hell is going on out there, Cal?" the president asked.

"Madam President. This is Agent Riley Barnes. She's been trying to answer that question all morning."

"Ms. Barnes, can you tell me why a dragon ripped apart Las Vegas and half of San Diego is now under water?"

Riley stood and cleared her throat. She hit a few buttons on the keypad on the table, and a spiraling wavelength materialized over the conference table. Van assumed it was a sensor log of the singularity. She described the timing and scope of the three breaks from the day before.

"These dwarf not only the breaks we've experienced but all of our theoretical models about how big they could actually get," Riley said.

"What made the tsunami?"

"The third break, we believe. It displaced a massive amount of the sea floor."

"And the dragons?"

Riley shook her head. "We don't know what they are or where they came from, of course. Dragon seems to be the most apt term we can apply to them. But it's clear that the breaks were of sufficient size to pull them here, from... well, it could be anywhere."

The president sat back in her chair. Her auburn hair was pulled into a tight bun and she wore a navy blue suit, accented by an American flag pin and some pearls around her neck. Her face mostly filled the screen, but Van could see that she was in some kind of command center, flanked by computer screens and military aides.

"Why were these breaks so big?"

Riley hit a few more buttons on the control pad, and the diagram floating above the table started moving. "Well," she said. "I'm not 100 percent on this, but it looks as though something happened and the singularity, has... it's grown."

"Grown?"

"Yes. We're talking on a nanoscale here, but, the change in its size has exponentially increased its disruptions. We were expecting this, being that the containment unit is fractured. Just not this soon. And... it's still happening."

"It's still growing?"

"Yes ma'am."

Cal sat, his eyes low. Van looked back and forth between the two of them.

"So what does this mean, exactly? How big is it going to get?"

"It means, the breaks will continue. They'll be bigger and more frequent. Alien incursions will only get worse, to the point that we'll eventually be overwhelmed. But…" She, too, dropped her gaze. The president leaned forward in her chair. Finally, Riley looked up. "The incursions aren't our real problem. If we can't halt the singularity's growth, it'll become so big that it will pull the planet apart. It'll destroy us."

7

It was just after 3 a.m., 3:02 and twenty-three seconds, to be exact, and Van was just getting home. He'd been in El Cajon for hours, dealing, on his own, with an "atmospheric disturbance" that had frozen everyone in a four-block radius. Cal, Ben and Riley, were out doing the same, fighting breaks scattered throughout the region.

He sat down on the edge of his bed and scrolled through the few calls he'd missed while out: his bank trying to sell him credit monitoring, his insurance adjuster about the car that had been swallowed along with Fiesta Island (could he explain, just one more time, what had happened, she wondered?) and his good friend, Kyle Owens, inviting him to a memorial service for the tsunami victims, at Sinclair's church.

"Oh, and don't forget to bring Riley," he said in the voicemail. "We sure loved her."

At least he wouldn't have to go it alone. After getting Cal's okay the next morning, he called Riley and broke the news to her. She made it a point to say how horribly put out she'd be by the arrangement, that she couldn't imagine anything worse than being trapped in church, for an entire evening, with Kyle and Katie Owens. That was a punishment she wouldn't wish on anyone, even Kyle and Katie Owens themselves.

"So you'll go?"

"Consider it a selfless act of valor."

"Maybe we'll get lucky and spacetime will tear open and swallow us before we get there, instead of after."

"Yeah, that'd be cool."

First Christian Church in Point Loma reminded Van of a castle. Two triangular bulwarks flanked the front entrance, an arch that crowned a set of plank doors. Someone had propped them open and put a smiling man and woman on each side. Above the door, the building climbed up another two stories, ending in a wavy, Spanish tile roof topped with a three-pronged bell tower.

Van and Riley walked hand-in-hand up to the entrance. One of the smiling people handed them a piece of paper describing, event-by-event, the night's service. Riley called it a bulletin. Inside, the church looked like most Van had seen. Rows of pews led up to an ornately decorated pulpit in the front, backed by a large cross on the wall.

Katie Owens spotted them immediately. She waved and

flashed a smile that Van was sure could do real damage if she wasn't careful with it. He squeezed Riley's hand, gritted his teeth and headed her way. When they got within arms length, she squealed and gave Riley a hug.

"Kyle and I are just so glad you all made it." Then, as if on cue, her face turned appropriately grim. "I'm so glad you're both okay. We were worried."

"We're glad, that.. you're both fine as well," Riley said.

Katie's smile snapped back into place. "Come on, I've got so many people I want to introduce you to!"

First Christian Church was a veritable who's who of San Diego. Just like at the party months earlier, they spent the next fifteen minutes being dragged about the room, meeting everyone and their kids, from school teachers to businessmen to lawyers, to... Councilwoman Zora. Van braced himself for a chilly reception, but got a warm greeting and smile instead. She told him how good it was to see him again. Even used his name, which Van was sure he hadn't ever given her.

"You're a member of the Rev. Sinclair's church?" Van asked.

"No, but my district has been one of the hardest hit over the last few months, I thought it important I be here."

"Last few months?" Riley asked.

"First there was the earthquake that destroyed the warehouse district, the second earthquake that swallowed Fiesta Island and now a tsunami. If I didn't know better, I'd say we were marching toward doomsday."

She said that last word — doomsday — with such pointed emphasis that Van almost flinched. He and Riley exchanged glances; even Katie's smile lapsed for nearly three full seconds.

"Well," Katie said, finally. "Let's hope not! If you'll excuse us, Councilwoman." She took them both by the arm, and continued pushing them around the room. Kyle joined them mid-stream with a smile bigger than his wife's, but without an explanation as to where he'd been. Finally, when Van felt as though he couldn't shake another hand, the pianist started to play, and Kyle and Katie ushered them to a pew near the front.

"I've never been to church on a Saturday," Riley said to Katie, as they were taking their seats.

"We actually do have a normal service on Saturday evenings," Katie said. "That's when we usually come anyway. The Sunday services are so busy, it's easier to find a parking spot. And Kyle likes to sleep in." She said that last part in a whisper and a with grin, as though she were telling Riley something very naughty.

The service began and they sang, they prayed, they lit candles, people took to the pulpit to talk about the lives lost and God's will, Councilwoman Zora gave a rousing speech about hope and perseverance and small government, as if that was somehow relevant, and then they tossed some dollars in the offering plate. Van didn't carry cash, but Riley had a twenty. Then, though, the Reverend Sinclair got up to preach. He was a little more fire and brimstone than Van had anticipated, especially for a memorial service, but the congregation lapped it up. Spontaneous shouts and Amens! were apparently quite acceptable, as were cheers and clapping. Sinclair preached on a passage from the Bible that seemed to promise God's enemies would get what was coming to them. And to hear Sinclair tell it (and his congregation agree), God had a lot of enemies. He went through the list: terrorists, liberals, gays, atheists — it seemed to Van there was hardly anyone on God's side. And somehow, each of these groups seemed to be jointly and single-handedly responsible for the tsunami.

"I have seen them, men who would destroy God!" Sinclair shouted. His face was red and beads of sweet had formed under his eyes and on his brow. "Men who would tear him down, who worship the wicked! Men who meddle with powers they do not understand, men who meddle with the forbidden arts, men who bend and break time as if they were gods themselves!"

This time, Van really did flinch. He glanced at Riley. She looked as horrified as he felt. "The dragon stood on the shore of the sea and it was a sign, a sign that the end is near! God promises these men, these evil, wicked men will see his judgment! They will bring destruction on themselves!"

As quickly as it began, it ended; Sinclair reached a fever-pitch, then settled into a solemn, closing prayer. Across the congregation, hands folded across laps and eyes closed. Van felt whiplashed; he resisted the impulse to grab Riley's hand and run. They had to do this in an orderly fashion.

As the prayer ended, the congregation stood and spontaneously burst into song, *The Doxology*, a hymn Van remembered from when his aunt and uncle had taken him to church as a boy. He took hold of Riley's hand, ready to bolt as soon as the opportunity arose, but Councilwoman Zora thwarted their exit with a beeline to their pew.

"Dr. Jacobs, do you have a moment?" she asked. "I wanted to speak with you about something."

Kyle and Katie excused themselves to say goodbye to some friends, and the councilwoman continued without waiting for Van to answer. "I did a little research, after we met on the beach that morning. I have to admit, I was very curious about you."

Van looked at Riley, but kept his face in check.

"It seems you had a problem with your past employer. A lawsuit? There are charges pending before the medical board, correct?"

"Are we rounding to a point, Councilwoman?"

"You didn't respond to the complaint and your hospital has declined to represent you. The court is poised to enter a default judgment and I'm inquiring as to your intentions on behalf of the plaintiffs. They're—"

"In your district?

She nodded.

"Isn't that a job for their attorney?"

"That's why I wanted to speak with you. Seems he's gone missing."

"Missing?"

"They haven't heard from him since he filed the paperwork." She paused, for obvious effect. "Didn't the San Diego Police question you, in connection with a murder just after you lost your privileges at Hillcrest General?"

Van had clearly underestimated the councilwoman. He searched for words, but nothing came. Riley didn't have the same trouble. "The city is in ruins," she said. "Hundreds of thousands are dead, even more have lost their homes. Surely you have more important things to worry about?"

"That's just it, Ms. Barnes. I'm not entirely sure that all these things aren't connected."

Before either of them could think of a response, Kyle and Katie interrupted. "Everything all right?" Kyle asked.

"Everything is just fine, Mr. Owens. But I do have to be going," Zora said. "Dr. Jacobs, if you think of anything that you'd like talk with me about, I'd love to hear from you." She said it with a smile, but the glare in her eyes sent an unmistakably different message. Zora fired the first shot, but Van was sure he didn't want the war. After she left, Kyle insisted they stay for a moment to visit with the Reverend.

"This'll just take a moment," Kyle said. "He was so excited when he heard you were coming, I know he wants to welcome you personally."

Van looked at Riley, then back at Kyle and Katie.

"Okay," Van said, "if it'll just be a moment."

"Fantastic!" Kyle said. He led them out of the pew and down the center aisle, then through a door at the back of the sanctuary. Compared to the frenzy out front, the back rooms were like tombs, dark and empty. Van and Riley followed the Owens down a long hallway covered in carpet so thick it swallowed their footsteps. Light spilled from a room at the far end. When they reached it, Kyle stepped to the side and ushered them in. Sinclair sat behind a desk, absorbed in writing in a spiral notebook. When he saw Van and Riley, his face brightened into a smile.

Van's stomach tightened.

Sinclair stepped from around the desk to shake their hands.

"I am so glad to see you two," he said. "So glad." He perched himself on the front edge of his desk, and let the room settle into an uncomfortable silence. His gaze locked on Riley, then he trained it on Van.

"So," he said finally, "what did you think of the service, Van?"

He thought carefully about his words. "It was… great. We…," he looked at Riley, "we really appreciated it. Thank you, for inviting us."

More silence. Sinclair folded his arms across his chest, looked down at his shoes and then shuffled back behind the desk to his chair.

"I would've thought you'd have hated it," he said, almost laughing. "But, I am glad that you enjoyed yourselves. All things considered. Can I offer you a drink?"

Van shook his head. "Actually, we can't stay long."

Sinclair's smile vanished. "Oh, I'm sorry to hear that, Van. I was hoping we'd have more time to talk."

Kyle and Katie's smiles had vanished, too. Van took a step back. "Maybe another time." He turned to Riley. "Ready, hon?"

"Actually," she said, "I was thinking that we should stay a while."

"What?"

She picked up a paperweight off Sinclair's desk and cracked Van across the head with it. He stumbled backwards and toppled over a chair, then hit the floor with a thud. The last thing he saw before he blacked out was Riley, standing over him, glaring.

The world rushed at Van, rousing him. How long had he been unconscious? He couldn't move his hands — they were tied to something. The wall? He tasted blood in his mouth. Wherever he was, it was cold and damp and he couldn't see anything. Mildew, he smelled mildew. Basement. They'd locked him in the basement. He tried to stand, but his feet were tied, too. Not just tied, shackled. They'd actually shackled him. Where do you even buy shackles? Is there like, a Web site? He settled back to a sitting position, resolved that he wasn't going anywhere.

Fifty-three minutes later, a door at the top of a set of stairs across the room creaked open and a flood of light spilled into the basement. Then, he heard the click of stiletto heals bounding down his way. When she was close enough, Van caught the unmistakable floral assault of Katie Owens' perfume. She walked toward him, bent over and put a warm washcloth to his forehead to clean the dried blood away. Then, without a word, she left, her heels clicking as she went.

It was another 83 minutes before Kyle came to see him. He brought Riley with him.

"How are you feeling Van?" Kyle asked as they came down the stairs.

"Betrayed." He leveled a pointed look at Riley when he said it. She didn't respond.

"Now, now," Kyle said. "We've brought you dinner." He set a plate of food and some water on the floor, then unlocked the shackles that held Van's arms to the wall. It felt good to put his hands down, but damned if he was going to eat anything they put in front of him.

"So tell me," Van said. "Are you garden variety lunatics or

is there some special reason you've locked me in the basement?"

"That's very good, Van. Never break cover, right?"

"What are you talking about?"

"Oh, you don't know? Why don't you ask your partner here? She's filled us in on what the lot of you have been up to over the last few months."

"I don't know what she's been telling you, but I wouldn't trust her. Anymore."

"Come on Van," Riley said. "Don't take it personally."

"Why did you do this?"

"Because the Reverend Sinclair is right," she hissed. "Station cannot be allowed to continue."

"You can't be serious."

"I left the FBI to follow Cal and his delusion of relevance in the grand scheme, and look at my reward. I'm a sodding cripple."

"You're alive, which is more than I can say for a lot of people in this city."

"Van," Kyle said. "She came to us."

"So, what? She's become a vital part of the organization in just a month or so?"

"Let's just say that bringing you in has endeared her to the leadership."

"Boys, boys. Can we move on please?" Riley asked. "What's done is done, Van. We've got more important things to talk about."

"Like?"

"Your access codes to Station's mainframe," Kyle said.

Van tried to adjust himself to a more comfortable position on the floor, with little success, being that his legs were still shackled. He was tired and nauseated and worried about just how hard Riley had hit him. "What do you need my codes for? Why not just use Riley's?"

Neither answered him.

"Ah, right. Because my codes are the only ones that can lock everyone else out." As chief medical officer, Van could override Cal, if he had good reason to believe Cal wasn't medically fit for duty or couldn't make decisions. He shook his head. "God, you're stupid."

"I beg your pardon?"

"Maybe Riley didn't tell you this, but the mainframe's controls are biometrically encoded. You can take my codes but they won't get you very far."

"Riley did inform us of that hurdle. But she also said your hand is likely to work whether or not it's still attached to your arm."

Touché. He looked at Riley. "What's the end game here? What are you trying to do?"

"Don't ask me," Riley said. "My job was to bring you here."

Van laughed, then shook his head. "You've cast your lot in with these people and you don't even know what the big plan is?"

"Enjoy your dinner, Van."

They left, but Riley glanced his way one last time as they reached the top of the stairs. He didn't see her again for quite a while, as the same scene repeated over days: Kyle would come down the stairs, usually alone, sometimes with people he didn't recognize, and demand Van's access codes. Van would refuse, and they'd leave. Sometimes they got a little rough, they'd hit him or throw freezing water on him and leave him shivering in his wet clothes, or tie him to the wall with his hands in the air for hours on end, but Van had learned to steel his mind against physical abuse back at the CIA. Not that he was enjoying himself. When Riley finally did come back with Kyle, almost four days later to the second, Van decided he'd had enough.

"What's up, traitor," he said when he saw her.

"You watch your place, boy," Kyle said.

"Boy? I'm three years older than you, you freak. God, Riley. I really thought you were smarter than this. You can't believe these morons will get away with any of this."

"We got you, didn't we?" Kyle said.

"Crowning achievement. You turned my weak-minded partner who sucker-punched me with a paperweight." He turned to Riley. "Did you give up Cal? Did you get him shot?"

Her eyes grew wide, and she shook her head. "I had nothing to do with that."

"Sure. Sinclair's merry band of lunatics figured it out all on their own."

"You mock things you don't understand, Van," Kyle said.

"You fear things you don't understand. The minute something comes along that challenges your world view you try and destroy it."

"Shut up."

"Wow. What a comeback. You got anything better than Cletus, here, Riley?"

"I said shut up!" Kyle screamed.

"Or what? You'll chain me to a wall and beat me?"

"We will end you! Starting with that Babylon under the ocean!"

"The ship? You're going to try and destroy the ship?"

"Not try, Van. Not try."

"How?"

His face turned grim, probably realizing he'd already said too much. "Just know that we can. And will."

Van looked at Riley. "Not that this hasn't been fun, but do you think that's everything?"

She nodded. "I think that's everything he knows." Kyle turned toward her, mouth slack-jawed and eyes wide. Riley hit him, knocking him against the wall. He slid to the floor, unconscious. She shook her hand. "Damn that hurts."

"You should've brought your paperweight," Van said.

"I'm so sorry." She pulled a set of keys from Kyle's pocket and then unshackled Van's feet. She pulled his comm from her pocket and his gun from a holster on her ankle and handed both back to him. She helped him stand, a taxing feat. "I hit you too hard. The paper weight was a lot heavier than I thought it would be, but by the time I picked it up, I was already committed."

"Don't worry about it."

"What did they do to you? They wouldn't let me come back until they were convinced I could extract the codes from you quicker than they could. I don't think they expected you to resist so long."

"It was nothing, I promise."

She didn't look convinced.

"Riley, I'm okay. All part of the plan, remember?"

She nodded. It was his idea for Riley to approach Kyle separately, play the part of disaffected defector, a scheme he hatched back when they'd first identified Kyle as the owner of the gun that shot Cal. He'd argued that they'd be suspicious and resistant to a traditional undercover approach, that the only chance of success was to play them from both ends. The injury to her leg was serendipitous, for lack of a better word, in that it finally convinced them she really was a bitter turncoat.

"Are Cal and the others, ready?

"Tactical team's been on standby for days. I just have to give them the green light." She looked back at Kyle. "God, do you know how long I've wanted to hit him?"

"Really? You want to hit him again?"

She considered it for a moment. "Nah. Maybe next time though. What do we do with him?"

"Shackle him."

"What are you going to do?"

"I'm going to go have a little chat with the Reverend."

By the time Van made it upstairs, the tactical team had already fanned through the sanctuary. They signaled each other with silent hand motions, moving in near lock-step coordination. A few days ago, Van would've called it overkill. Most of Sinclair's people were desk trained and probably didn't even know they were involved in anything more than a soul crushing church. That was before they tortured him and kept him shackled in a basement for days.

Ben and Cal came in behind the tactical team. When Ben spotted Van, he came running over. "You okay?" he asked.

Van nodded. "Where's Sinclair?"

"Let's go find out."

They headed for the back of the church, and then down the hallway. The second half of the tactical team had come from the rear and quickly took up positions throughout the administrative rooms. They held in place, waiting for Ben and Van to meet them outside Sinclair's office. Ben gave the signal and they kicked through the door.

Sinclair, though, was gone.

They seized a trove of documents from Sinclair's office, including an entire file drawer about Cal. As best as any one could tell, they'd been stalking him for the better part of a year. Why Sinclair chose that night at the hospital to finally take him out, they still didn't know. Nor did they find anything in the files that told them exactly how Sinclair had come to know who Cal was and what he did. Kyle wasn't helpful either. He'd stopped talking when he woke up in one of Station's holding cells, a first for him on both counts.

And they'd made a big slip-up taking computers from the church. Sinclair had armed the doors to the offices with magnetic degaussing rings so that the hard drives scrambled as they were carried out. Carlos said he'd do what he could to try and recover as much data as possible, but that "no one should hold their gut" — his words.

"You know," Ben said to Van, as they sat in the conference room pouring through documents, "Sinclair had to let Kyle in on the fallback plan. He has to know where they are, or, at least, have a really good idea of where we should start looking."

Van agreed. He was about to say something about how lucky

Sinclair and Katie were, deciding to flee the church just as the raid was about to begin. Instead he started coughing. Ben poured a glass of water from a pitcher on the table and passed it his way.

"Sounds like you're choking up a lung."

Dr. Bower had called him twice about scheduling his surgery. A few operating rooms in town were finally up and running again, but only for priority cases. He could, though, pull some strings and get Van in quickly, he said.

"I'm okay."

"Why don't you go home and sleep. Come back tomorrow."

"Too much to do."

He sifted through the documents in front him, then through a box sitting beside his chair on the floor. He found the book Kyle had kept locked in his safe, the one that said *Coram Deo* on the spine. While they were at the church, a separate team had raided the Owens' house. The book was mostly a bunch of religious rambling, from what he could see. It probably didn't have much intelligence, but it might have another use.

"Where you going?" Ben asked.

"To make the caged bird sing."

Station's brig was on the lowest sub-level, the third below the parking garages. Van had never had any reason to venture down that far before. In fact, the brig was just one of quite a few parts of Station he'd never seen. Some had been locked down — and presumably empty — for years before his time. Others, he'd just never made it to, or found. The place was like a labyrinth.

The brig, though, was about as he expected. It had just four cells, one off each corner. They were secured with electromagnetic fields, marked only by tiny blue dots of energy that floated across the doorframes. Kyle lay on the floor in the cell farthest from Van, with his back turned. He rolled over and sat up on the bench along the wall when he heard footsteps. His grin, amazingly, was still intact.

Van crossed his arms and stared. Kyle clapped. "Bravo," he said.

"Where are they Kyle?"

"Who's that now?"

"Why are you protecting them? They abandoned you."

"You're wrong."

"Really? I mean, you'd think your wife would've at least tried to look for you before she took off with Sinclair. They ran and didn't even look back." Kyle fell suddenly stoic. He looked away. Van pressed on: "You don't think there's anything between the two of them, do you?"

"Fuck you."

Van laughed. "Wow, that was easier than I expected. Maybe you've already had that same thought? You know, I barely recognize you without that stupid grin on your face."

Kyle locked eyes with Van. "You have no idea what's happening here."

He showed Kyle the book. "Maybe I can read all about it."

"That book is beyond you."

"How did Sinclair find out who Cal was? How did he know he'd be at the hospital?"

"We celebrated, the night Cal died. It was a glorious moment. One we've waited long for."

"He's alive, wingnut."

Kyle's mouth fell open. He stammered. "You're lying."

Van shrugged. "Whatever. I really don't care if you believe me."

Kyle stood and walked toward the edge of his cell. He stood inches from Van, the two of them separated only by a humming energy field. "Don't you understand what we're trying to do? We're not the bad guys."

"If you're not, then who is?"

"Why don't you ask your friend Cal, if he's still alive as you say he is."

"I'm pretty sure I know what he'll say."

"You trust him?"

The question caught Van off guard. "Of course."

"Why? Has he answered all your questions? What do you really know about this place you're in? What do you know about that ship?"

"Enough."

"Then why were they here?"

"What are you talking about?"

"When the aliens crashed. What were they doing here?"

Van stood for a moment, watching Cal work quietly in his office. Kyle was an asshole, but he'd asked questions Van didn't have good answers to.

"Sorry we didn't get Sinclair," Van said, popping his head through Cal's door.

"We'll get him." Cal shuffled some papers and put them away in a file folder, which he shut up in his drawer. He always hurried to pull something off his desk and put it out of sight when Van walked in. "You'll never believe this," he said, "but the tactical team found a tunnel built into the fireplace. That's probably how he got out without us seeing him."

Van sat down in front of Van's desk and let out a long sigh. "A tunnel? Who are these people?"

Cal shrugged. "Well, it gets better. The tunnel led down through Point Loma to a sea cave just under Cabrillo. They'd built a boat dock. We've frozen his bank accounts, seized all of his assets that we could find, and the rest, I'm hoping, we'll find after we finish going through his files. He'll have to surface sooner or later."

"He knows—"

"Too much. I know."

"If it's any consolation, I think he wants us to be kept as secret as we do."

"Maybe."

Van leaned back in the chair and took a long leisurely look at the ceiling of Cal's office. Then at the wall on his right, and all the pictures Cal had hung on the left. After that, he found the gray Berber carpet extremely interesting.

"Van?"

He looked up, met Cal's gaze. "How did he find you?"

"If I knew that we'd probably be having a very different conversation."

"You have no ideas? No theories?"

Cal shook his head.

"Would you tell me, if you did?"

Cal smiled, and then told Van he'd see him in the morning.

Van took the hint.

8

Van floated in the Pacific, staring at an empty sky. The water swelled underneath him as waves rolled toward the shore. Kids squealed on the beach, seagulls squawked in the air and nearby surfers chatted about the calm waters, all as fresh, salty air filled his lungs. He felt, for a moment, he could sleep, until a rough wave rocked him to his side. The sun grew bright, blinding. Pain pierced his skull. He heard someone call his name. The water grew cold and choppy. He started to sink.

"Van… Van?"

Everything was harsh and grey. His throat was on fire. A man stood over him, repeating his name and shining a bright light in his eyes. The world came into focus, the lights over head, the ugly green tile walls, the clatter of people in the background. His head ached and felt heavy. His body didn't want to move. He shifted uncomfortably against the rough, industrial sheets lining his hospital bed. The man standing over him smiled.

"How do you feel?" he asked.

Van didn't answer.

"You had a reaction to the Propofol, anesthesia had a hard time bringing you back."

"Reaction?" His voice was dry. It hurt to talk.

"Nothing to worry about right now. Other than that, everything went well. We got a good tissue sample. We'll move you to a room soon."

Van wanted nothing to do with a room, but couldn't keep his eyes open long enough to argue. When he woke again, he'd already been moved and settled in. The sun outside was setting. He sat up, slowly, trying to gauge how weak the biopsy had left him. Despite a hole drilled into his skull, the procedure was supposed to be outpatient. He should've been home in his own bed by now, and he argued the point with everyone who came to his room that evening: the surgeon, Dr. Bower, the charge nurse. But his reaction to the anesthesia, they all said, was reason enough for him to at least spend the night.

He'd told Cal, though, that he needed just a day to attend a friend's funeral. With so many dead after the tsunami, it was a good cover. But, that meant he had to be out of the hospital and back to work the next morning. There was no way he could lie overnight, taking up a bed for no good reason that he could see. After the surgeon left and the nurse coming on for the night shift stopped in to check on him, he made up his mind. He swung his feet over the bed, got his clothes out of the closet, dressed and sneaked out of the hospital.

The next morning, Van woke to a dozen voicemail messages. Most were from the hospital, two were from Dr. Bower. He sat up slowly, his head pounding, whether from the surgery or just another headache, he couldn't tell. He also felt sick to his stomach. Moving made the room spin.

He showered and dressed. His dry cleaner, and presumably most of the clothes he'd sent there two weeks earlier, were still under water, so he had to wear an older sports coat that didn't really fit well. He picked out a button up shirt to match and a pair of dark jeans. Breakfast was an afterthought, but he forced himself to down a piece of plain toast and half a glass of skim milk. An hour after waking, he was in his car and heading toward Station. The bulk of the flood waters had receded, but there were quite a few roads downtown still closed or just too torn up to be safe. Those that were open were jammed with cars. He considered getting out and walking more than once.

As soon as he arrived, Cal asked about the funeral. Van avoided eye contact and mumbled something about it being a pretty typical service. He tried to change the subject and remarked that spacetime seemed to have remained intact — relatively — during his day away.

"We've engaged a contingency plan."

"Contingency?"

"Electromagnetic field generators, in the water. EM fields refract the temporal energy coming out of the singularity and the water's conductive, so it magnifies the effect. While you were playing hostage, we've been slowly putting that into place."

"Why was this only a contingency plan?"

"Because it's our last plan. It's a bandage. For every new generator we place, the singularity burns out two of the old ones."

Van looked around. Station was as deserted as he'd ever seen it. He didn't hear Riley's laugh or Ben's constant tapping on the monitors.

"Where is everyone?"

"City Heights. Pretty substantial break there about four this morning and reports of strange animals prowling the streets. Sounds like a couple class twos got through."

"You should've called me."

"I wanted you to take the time you needed."

Van sighed. "I'll join them."

He turned to leave, but Cal called out. "You doing okay? You look kind of tired."

Van rubbed the back of his head. He'd taken the bandage off when he woke up in the morning, but still, he knew he looked awful. His skin was pale, he had circles under his eyes.

"I didn't sleep well. I'll check in with Riley and Ben and give you an update when I get out there, okay?"

Cal nodded. Van considered, for just a moment, telling him everything, telling him the truth. But, he didn't know what the truth was, yet. He nodded back and then left for City Heights.

Van found Riley and Ben on a sidewalk outside an abandoned house, just on the east side of the 15 Freeway and not far off University Avenue. City Heights was a small neighborhood that, for many years, gentrification had forgotten. It'd only recently seen an influx of richer and, as it were, whiter people, but signs of its past poverty still lingered. Its one advantage was that it was higher above sea level than most of San Diego, so it emerged from the tsunami relatively unscathed. Ben spotted him approaching.

"You look horrible," he said.

"Good to see you, too."

"Sorry, I just… you okay?"

Van nodded. "What's going on?"

Riley looked him over, then glanced between him and Ben and apparently decided not to add her own assessment of Van's appearance. "Solid class twos, came through a break about four blocks over. Created quite a crater in the middle road. We've been telling people it's a sinkhole."

"How many?"

"We think four or five, judging from the spatial distortions we're getting," Ben said. "We've tracked them here."

They proceeded through the front gate and up to the house. It was an old Craftsman style bungalow, two stories. The windows were boarded over and weeds had overtaken the front yard. The porch creaked as they walked toward the door, weapons ready. Ben reached for the handle, but the door swung open when he touched it. Probably hadn't been locked in years.

The house was gloomy inside and stank of sewage. Van though, detected a faint spicy odor, a smell he'd come to hate. In front of them, a set of stairs led up to the second floor. The remnants of a living room sat to their left and a dining room to the right. The kitchen was probably back behind that, Van thought. Ben pointed off in both directions, giving him and Riley the signal to fan out and cover the first floor. Van took to the dining room, a narrow space with a long table in the center that at one time was probably a point of pride for its owners. Now, it was covered in a permanent layer of grime and had just three legs. An old china hutch stood against the far wall. It was empty. The chandelier was gone. Van scanned the room, but saw no signs that anything had been disturbed for years.

He moved on to the kitchen. The lower cabinets and old tile counter were still there, but at some point, the upper cabinets had collapsed and were now piles of broken wood. Like the dining room, nothing seemed out of place. He was about to double-back and find the others when something dropped on him from the ceiling. He hit the ground, and after a herculean effort, managed to roll over to see a snarling ball of fur, teeth and saliva on top of him. He couldn't make out all its features, but it was big, leaden and had at least four limbs, all of which were firmly wrapped around his body. It opened its mouth and showed Van rows of long, dripping teeth. He pried his arms loose in time to grab its jaws and hold it back, but it thrashed against him.

Then, he heard a loud pop, followed by a yelp. The thing collapsed on his chest and Van looked up to see Ben standing over him, gun still smoking. Riley came running into the room.

"Get this off me, please," Van said.

Ben helped Van to his feet. "It get a jump on you?"

"Literally. It was climbing on the ceiling."

In unison, Ben and Riley looked up, then back at Van. He bent over to inspect the dead alien on the floor. It looked like a dog. A mean, snarling, violent beast of a dog, but a dog nonetheless.

"Let's stay together," Ben said. "Don't hesitate to—"

Riley fired her gun at one of the alien dogs, behind them. It took the bullet in the chest and tumbled over before sliding head first into the dining room wall.

"—shoot."

"Two down," Riley said.

They went upstairs, one by one, with Ben in the lead. They all kept one eye in front and one eye on the ceiling. The landing at the top of the stairs was small, and it opened up to two bedrooms and a bathroom. Ben cleared the bathroom, then he took the left bedroom while Van and Riley went to the right.

They took a quick look — the room was mostly empty except for what was left of an old metal bed frame — and saw nothing. "Maybe they took off when we started shooting," Van said.

That's when another dog burst through the floorboards and lunged at Riley. She stumbled backward. Van picked it off with two well placed shots, but before he could even ask if she was okay, another dog exploded through the wall behind him. It hit him in the back and knocked him to the floor. With his last bit of strength, he kicked it into a corner. Riley fired until her gun clicked empty and it lay bleeding and motionless on the floor.

Ben appeared in the door and he looked at Van on the floor, the broken wall and floorboards, the two dead alien dogs and Riley with her gun still raised.

"I'm always late to the party," he said.

"I think that might be all of them."

Van tried to push himself up, but his legs wouldn't work. He went down again, this time with a loud thump as his head cracked the floor. Riley and Ben ran to his side, but he waved them off.

"I'm okay. Really." He tried to stand again, again unsuccessfully.

"All right, that's enough," Ben said. He bent down and put Van's arm across his shoulders and helped him up, then downstairs and out to the sidewalk. "I'm driving you home," he said.

"I'll be fine."

"Obviously not."

"You can barely stand," Riley said. "Did one of them hurt you?"

"I've just not been sleeping well, that's all." They weren't buying it. It was partly true, though. He just wasn't saying why he hadn't been sleeping well. He looked at the two of them, their arms crossed and staring at him like he was death, ready for a grave.

"Freeze! Hands in the air!"

They turned. Behind them, the two detectives who'd interrogated Van at the hospital crouched by the doors of a unmarked car, guns pointed. "Toss out your weapons and hands in the air, now!" the taller one shouted.

Van, Riley and Ben tossed their guns to the ground, and then slowly raised their hands. The detectives came forward, slowly, with guns still raised, and then tied off their hands behind their backs with cobra cuffs. After they were secured, Councilwoman Zora stepped out from the back seat of their car.

"I had a private investigator following Dr. Jacobs," Zora said, offering an explanation no one had asked for. "When he saw the three of you go in that house with guns, he phoned me. I called the detectives."

Before he could say anything, Van's comm vibrated in his pocket. Then Riley's blared, as did Ben's. They glanced at each other, then to the Councilwoman.

"What is that?" she asked.

"You might want to unleash our hands," Riley said.

"What is happening?" Zora asked, again.

"I want to tell you, but you need to have the Hardy Boys here untie me."

As Riley argued with Zora and the detectives, the wind picked up, blowing down instead of across. A dark cloud spread out above them, throwing a shadow along the ground. It drew everyone's attention; Riley and Zora fell silent and looked up, the detectives' hands went instinctively for their weapons. Sprinkles of sand landed in Van's eyes.

"I think we should not be here," he said.

More sand fell, just a few specks at first, then a downpour.

They ran, but Riley's leg gave out and she tumbled. Van turned back, but he couldn't loosen his restraints enough to help her. Walls of sand crashed around them, burying the two detectives and knocking Van to his ass. He lost sight of Ben and Councilwoman Zora. He scrambled to his knees and crawled over to Riley, staying low enough that she could get a grip on his shoulder. She latched on and he pushed himself to his legs, dragging Riley to hers at the same time. Blinded and choking, they hobbled through the falling sand, trying to find the detectives' car. Just when Van thought they wouldn't make it, a hand reached through the falling sand and grabbed Van by the arm. It was Zora; she pulled him to the edge of the car and then shoved him through the driver's door. Ben was already in the passenger's seat. Then, she went back for Riley.

So many seconds ticked off. Sand poured through the open

doors, covering Van like a snowdrift. After an interminable amount of time, Riley burst into the backseat, head first. She landed with a thud, but quickly wiggled around to a sitting position so she could watch the door.

Van waited for Zora to follow, but she never came.

The sand piled high, sealing them in the car. Eventually silence fell, and everything settled. Ben twisted himself into a ball, a gymnastic attempt to get his hands in front of him. He succeeded, to Van's surprise, and then rummaged through the glove box until he found a set of police-issued clippers for their restraints. He freed himself, then Van and Riley.

Van settled into the seat, a pile of sand pinning his legs. He tried to gauge how much was on top of the car — its windshield had already cracked and the ceiling was buckling — and then how much oxygen the three of them had left. His chest tightened. Sweat trickled down his neck. Instinctively, he reached for the door handle and tried to force it open.

"Van, calm down," Ben said.

The ocean. He thought about the big, wide-open ocean with lots of space and fresh air. His jacket was too tight. He pulled it off, crumpled it into a ball and tossed it to the backseat. His muscles tensed. His shirt was too tight, too. He was about to rip it off when Ben reached across the seat and took his hand.

"Look at me," Ben said. "You have to calm down. Breathe, slowly." He squeezed, and Van squeezed back, hard. Their eyes met, and Van focused on taking controlled, steady breaths. After a few seconds, he settled again into his seat and closed his eyes. The ocean. Big, big ocean. Its waves rocked him back and forth, until he fell unconscious.

Cool air cascaded through the car. Van gasped, but his eyes wouldn't focus. He'd heard the windshield shatter, and then voices. Someone had grabbed him by his arms and he was moving through the air, rising, maybe? Sunlight blinded him. The moving stopped and he lay on the ground. He couldn't catch his breath.

"Van, can you hear me?" It was Cal, standing over him. He kneeled down and brought a bottle of water to Van's lips, which he gulped until it was half-empty.

"What happened?"

"Break. It brought the desert here."

Van pushed himself to a sitting position. To the north, and to the south, almost as far as he could see, the neighborhood was covered in sand so high it had swallowed houses and edged up the sides of tall buildings. About two dozen people stood around the hole he'd been pulled from, some holding shovels, others with pick axes. After a few more minutes, they'd pulled Ben out, and he lay resting on the sand beside Van. Riley came next, and then Councilwoman Zora's body. They had more trouble finding the two detectives.

"How much?" Van asked.

"About five square miles, twenty, thirty feet deep in some places. We're still getting data back from the satellites. We tracked you by your comms."

"How long were we under there?"

"You don't know?"

"I blacked out."

"About fifteen minutes, we think."

With Cal's help, Van stood. So much sand, everywhere. Three Humvees sat parked a couple hundred feet away, on top of a newly formed dune. "This is my fault," he said.

"What?"

"I should've stopped this. That's what you brought me on for."

"We're all working toward the same goal."

"Survivors?"

"We're mobilizing as many rescue teams as we can."

"Zora saved us. We wouldn't have made it without her." Van glanced over at her body. "What can we do?"

"Go home."

"Cal—"

"Go. Home."

Van wanted to argue, but but Ben shook his head. Cal was probably right, anyway. They weren't in any condition to help. They took one of the Humvees, and Ben drove. They dropped Riley first; her place in South Park was the closest. It took nearly another half-hour to make it downtown to Van's apartment. Flood-ravaged roads and a seemingly endless stream of cars trying to get out of the city slowed them considerably.

"I guess everyone's leaving," Ben said.

"Do you blame them?"

Ben pulled into Van's parking garage and parked the car. "I'm going to help you upstairs," he said.

"I'm fine."

"You don't look fine."

Surgery one day, buried alive the next. What could possibly be wrong? Regardless, he didn't have the energy to argue. Ben came around to his side, helped him out of the seat and then put Van's arm across his shoulders.

Upstairs, Ben led him to his couch. He had sand in his hair, his ears, his underwear. It was all very chaffing, and he wanted a shower. Ben stood, watching him.

"Maybe I should call a doctor," he said.

"I am a doctor."

"Then what's wrong with you?"

"It's just been a long couple of days. A long couple of months actually. Hell, a long couple of years. I need a drink."

"What?"

"Vodka? Whiskey." He went to the kitchen, where he kept some wine and liquor in the cabinet above the refrigerator. He grabbed a bottle of Johnny Walker Blue that he'd been saving, cracked it open and poured two shots.

"It's barely even two o'clock."

"I know what time it is. Drink."

They tossed back the shots, and Van immediately poured two more. Ben hesitated.

"The way things are going, do you really want to risk that being your last drink ever? I mean, you could walk out of here and the singularity could drop a mountain on you. Already dropped a desert on you."

Ben sighed, grabbed the shot and downed it. Van promptly refilled the glass, downed his own shot, then he poured himself another and took that one, too.

"You never told me how you do that," Ben said.

"Drink? I practice, a lot."

"The time thing. How you always know what time it is."

Van shrugged. "I was halfway through the first grade before I realized that other people couldn't do the time thing," he said.

"Nothing like being different to make for a fantastic childhood."

Ben turned to face the floor-to-ceiling windows that lined the west wall of Van's apartment. He'd furnished the place mostly with modern pieces he'd picked himself from a little boutique store in Mission Valley, but it was a 4,000 square foot penthouse, so even with a couple couches, chairs and a big dining table, it still looked open and sparse. Ben seemed taken with the ocean view.

Van refilled their glasses one more time, and then he joined Ben by the windows. After they drank, they stood quietly for a long while. The alcohol had settled nicely, and Van felt its buzz.

"You ever look back at where you've been in your life," he said, "and realize how much you've done wrong?"

Ben set his glass down. "You think you've done wrong?"

"The question, I think, is if I've done anything right."

"I know why you left training at the CIA. Is that what you're talking about?"

"No. Mostly, no."

"What has you taking stock all the sudden?"

"Ben, I need to tell you…" He searched for the right words. He wanted to tell Ben everything: about the headaches, about the MRI scans and the biopsy. But he couldn't bring himself to say it. He felt tears well in his eyes. "I—"

Ben reached out and put his hand on the side of Van's face. "It's okay," he said.

Then, he kissed him. After the shock faded, after he felt Ben's lips on his, he let his eyes close and he kissed back — but just for a moment. Reality dropped in and he backed away, nearly falling over one of the kitchen stools.

"God, I'm sorry," Ben said.

"No, no. It's, not a… it's okay." They stared at each other in silence until Van's cell phone rang. He pulled it from his pocked and glanced at the caller ID. It was Dr. Bower's office. Perfect timing. He hit the decline button.

"I should go," Ben said.

Van let him get all the way across the room and halfway out before he called out. "You don't have to," he said. Ben stopped, but didn't turn back. "You don't have to go."

After a few achingly long seconds, nine, exactly — Van counted — Ben stepped back inside and closed the door.

"You sure?"

Van nodded. "Yeah, I'm sure."

The clocked clicked to 6:00 a.m., and on cue, Van's eyes opened. He'd never needed an alarm, he just put it in his mind that he'd wake up at a certain time, and except for that night after the blob exploded, he always did. Six was earlier than normal, but he had a twofold mission: greet his good friend Kyle Owens for a chat before anyone else was around, and sneak out of the apartment before Ben — who was lying next to him in bed — woke up.

So when Kyle woke, Van was sitting, cross-legged, on the floor outside his cell.

"Morning, sunshine," Van said.

"How long have you been sitting there?"

"Fifteen minutes."

"Then this must be important." He sat up and backed himself against the wall. He flashed Van a grin.

"You're chipper for a man locked in a cage."

"What do you want, Van?"

"I'm still waiting for you to answer my questions about your wife and the good Reverend."

Kyle examined Van closely, then shook his head. "No."

"No? You're not going to answer?"

"No, that's not why you're really here."

Van locked eyes with Kyle. "What are you talking about?"

"Your fearless leader isn't the only one who recruits with a purpose."

Van stood. "Are you making some kind of sense?"

"Sinclair chose me just like Cal chose you."

"How do you know Cal chose me?"

"Why do you think we shot him that night, Van?"

Kyle was just full of surprises. "You were trying to stop him from meeting me?"

"Score one for the new kid."

"Why?"

Kyle shook his head. "You really have no idea what's going on here, do you?"

Van hit the controls on the wall beside Kyle's cell, and the field separating them dissolved. He stepped in close.

"Why don't you tell me?"

Kyle grinned. Van grabbed him by the throat and slammed into the wall. He held him there, seething. Kyle choked out a laugh, then strained himself to say: "Never pegged you for a temper." Van released him, stepped back and drew his gun. "What's this? Am I supposed to think you're going to shoot me, Van? Murder me in cold blood? You're not the type."

Van chambered a round. Kyle's grin disappeared. "This isn't the way it's supposed to be," he said.

"If you've got something to tell me, now would probably be a good time. I'm not going to let any more people die. Except maybe you."

Kyle stood silent. Van held himself steady, fighting his rage. Then, his phone buzzed. After a few seconds, he pulled it out with one hand and kept the gun on Kyle with the other. It was Dr. Bower's office again. His results had come back, and the nurse on the other end wanted to know when he could come in to talk about them?

Van took a long look at Kyle. He holstered his gun, told the nurse he'd be right over and relocked Kyle's cell.

"Don't go anywhere. We're not done."

The whole meeting with Dr. Bower took about fifteen minutes. Van didn't need the usual hand holding or long-winded explanations. He didn't need the false hope.

"Do you have any questions?" Dr. Bower asked him.

Van glanced down at the report he'd been handed. He didn't read it all, but caught a few key words. He handed it back, shook his head and then left.

Back at Station, Van ran into Ben, first. That was his luck.

"I wondered where you were," Ben said.

"Sorry about that. I had some stuff to do. I need to talk to Cal and Riley and… you, about something. Where are they?"

"I didn't plan for what happened last night. I want you to understand that."

"I know."

"I'm sorry—"

"There's nothing to apologize for."

"I know your not… I mean, I know you couldn't ever… could you?"

Van didn't answer. He didn't have an answer to give. Ben furrowed his brow and pursed his lips. "I think Cal and Riley are up in the conference room," he said.

They took the stairs up to the upper level and crossed the length of the catwalk. The trip took just forty-three seconds, but Van felt like they were wading through wet cement. As Ben had said, Riley and Cal were inside the conference room, going over some charts and graphs that reduced the subject at hand—likely their impending doom at the hand of an alien black hole—into pretty lines and curves. Van walked in first, then stood silently, looking at his feet and waiting for them to realize he'd entered. Finally, Cal looked up and saw them. He called them to the table.

"We might have some good news," he said. He went on, pointing out detail after detail on the charts and explained how the geometry of the EM field grid they'd created in the water had an unexpected effect on the singularity. Not only had the temporal energy radiating into local spacetime been reduced, but the total output escaping the singularity fluctuated — depending on exactly how the separate planes in the grid intersected — by something like a billionth of a percent up or down.

"It's some kind of destructive interference that we've never noticed before. Like, noise-canceling headphones," Riley said. Her smile lit up. It didn't sound like much to Van, but she and Cal were sure excited. "It'll take days to run the models but we might be able, you know, at the least buy ourselves some time that we didn't have before. It was Carlos, actually, who gave me the idea."

"Carlos?"

"His infrasound weapon. It got me thinking about sound-waves and you know how it goes when one theory just rolls into the next and suddenly you've got a solution."

Not really, but he nodded anyway. Cal looked up at the two of them, but Ben was staring at Van.

"Whoa, guys. Don't go crazy. It's just one of the biggest breakthrough we've had in years…"

"I wasn't at a funeral," Van said.

Cal and Riley glanced at each other, then at Ben, but he shrugged. The two of them straightened back in their chairs, and Ben leaned up against the doorframe.

"I was in the hospital. I'm sorry, for lying. I didn't want to say anything, until I knew…"

"Knew what?" Riley asked.

Van looked at his feet again, then at the ceiling, then back to his feet. "I have cancer."

Van looked back at Ben, but he was staring off, out the door. "The technical term is, well, it looks something like oligoden-droglioma, the biopsy wasn't conclusive, it's… it's a brain tumor. Usually pretty slow growing…"

"Usually?" Cal asked.

"Yeah. It's odd, actually. A few months ago, when I had my intake physical, here. There was no detectable sign of a tumor. I saw the CT scans myself. Now it's at four centimeters."

"That's big?" Riley asked.

"Huge. And the genetic markers, they're atypical. It's all very — it's all strange. Suspect."

"Van, what are you saying?" Cal asked.

Van shifted his weight from leg to leg. "It's possible... likely... that something I've been exposed to has either caused the cancer or accelerated the growth of something that was already there."

"Exposed to since...?"

"Since I joined Station."

Cal dropped his gaze. Tears formed in Riley's eyes, but she held it together. She looked down to Cal, then to Ben, then back to Van.

"Well, what's the treatment?" she asked.

Van felt like all the oxygen had been sucked out of the room. He hadn't anticipated tears. "Radiation, maybe chemo. The tumor spreads like... it has tentacles. Makes surgery impossible. The oncologists think that... that with any luck, I'll get a few more weeks."

Riley gasped.

"Weeks?" Ben asked.

Van looked back, and nodded. Ben crossed the room and took a seat, looking as though someone hit him with a baseball bat in the gut.

"I don't accept that," Cal said.

"There's nothing to accept or not accept. It's just how it is."

Ben started to say something, but fell silent instead. Van lingered another few seconds, making eye contact with each of them before leaving.

On the drive home, he burst into tears.

9

Riley stood at the door, but Van had no idea why.

"Oh. My. God," she said. He looked at her, slack-jawed. He'd woken only ten minutes earlier, and wasn't yet running at full speed. She stepped past him through the door and took straight across the room to the floor-to-ceiling windows.

"Why have you not had me over before?" she asked.

"Riley?"

"This is your flat? Unbelievable."

"Who let you up the elevator?"

"A very sweet young man working behind the front desk downstairs. I told him I was your sis' in for a visit."

"And he what, thought the accent was for effect?"

"You'll have to ask him." She looked around at the kitchen and patio outside, ran her hands across the back of the couch and then turned back to the windows. "Ben has always talked about buying a place like this, he'd love it."

Van's face flushed. "He's seen it. Actually."

"Oh. So what, there was a party I wasn't invit— Oh."

"There's no 'oh,' Riley."

"Of course."

"I'm serious. It was, there was—"

"I get it. Absolutely."

They both started talking at once, and then they stopped, neither stringing together a full sentence. Van shifted his wait uncomfortably from foot to foot. An awkward silence spread between them, a silence Van desperately wanted to fill. He started again: "Not that I mind, much, but what are you doing here?"

She laid her cane on the ottoman and took a seat on the couch. "You're due at the hospital this morning for treatment. And you shouldn't be doing that alone."

Van started to protest, but Riley interrupted. "Nuh uh. You see this face, it's resolved isn't it? You've seen it before."

Van nodded. He had seen it before.

"Then good, you know there'll be no use arguing with me." She checked her watch. "Not all the roads down here have been reopened and traffic's a bit of a nightmare so go on and get yourself ready or we'll be late. You can't very well go in your shorts."

"Riley... I'm not going to the hospital."

"What do you mean? Of course you are."

He shook his head. "I'm not starting treatment."

"I don't understand."

"I had a long talk with Dr. Bower yesterday and I've been staring at the imaging studies all weekend. Have you ever seen someone go through chemo, radiation? I don't want my last days to be like that. I don't want to die lying down. I want to fight, with all of you."

Tears welled in her eyes. "But, you said there is no chance you'll live without treatment—"

"There's no chance I'll live with it."

"I won't let you give up like this."

He sat beside her. "I'm not giving up. I've got one thing left I can do, and I won't get it done sitting in a hospital."

"What one thing?"

"Come with me."

He helped her up and took her to his den, down the hall, just beyond the bedroom. Stacks of papers and file boxes sat everywhere, covering the floor, his desk and all the chairs.

"This is all my research. Case studies, papers, databases, everything. Somewhere, in here, might still be the key to saving the world."

"God help us."

"Amen."

They spent the day holed up in Van's den. Riley had said — more than once — how impressed she was with his work. He'd designed a drug that could actually repair damaged neurons.

"That's the way it looks on paper, any way. I've not had the most success in my... limited trials."

She flipped through a stack of papers, "You've altered the transcription factor from the original design?"

He nodded. "Walter's idea, actually. I've had him modeling a series of controlled tests for weeks, analyzing millions of permutations. It's the best I could do."

He cradled his head in his hands. Riley sat silently for a few moments, staring at him. Then, in a small voice, she asked: "Does it hurt?"

"Only when my eyes are open."

She reached over and squeezed his hand. "I wish you'd reconsider treatment. Maybe I can take over from here, you've explained how the drug works and I think I've got a firm—"

"I've considered and reconsidered and then considered some more. This is for the best."

She pursed her lips. "Nothing says I've got to like it, though."

"You know, you should actually make an appearance at the office sometime before the day officially ends."

"I spoke with Cal this morning, before I came over. But, I do want to check in on Egon."

"Who the hell is Egon?"

"Oh... Egon... is the dragon."

"The what? You named it?"

"I visit it sometimes. Do you know if it's a boy or girl? I assumed boy."

"Riley."

"What? I thought it might get lonely. I like animals. I've got weimaraners."

"It's unconscious. And it's a dragon."

"I think it can hear me."

"You talk to it?"

"Sing. I sing to it... sometimes."

This, somehow, was completely reasonable in her mind. Van shook his head, and then pretended to flip through some files while he thought of a way to change the subject.

"Anyway, two of us out, all day long—"

"Three of us, actually."

"Three?"

She looked up, startled. "What?"

"You said three, who else is gone?"

"I said three?"

"Yes."

"Are you certain, because—"

"Riley!"

"Ben. Ben is out."

"Out where?"

She glanced sideways for a moment, then tried hard to avoid making eye contact. "On a case, I think? I'm going to have some tea. Would you like a cup?" She stood up and started out the room, toward the kitchen. Van called after her, and then got up to follow.

"What kind of case?"

"It's just a little thing really." She opened the pantry door and rummaged around until she found some loose leaf on the shelf. "You sure you don't want any?"

Van was about to force the conversation back on track when the doorbell rang. He eyed Riley carefully, then went for the door. It was Cal, carrying bags of fast food.

"You tell the front desk you were my sister, too?"

"Uncle."

"It's a regular family reunion." He shot a glance back at Riley, then moved to welcome Cal inside.

"Great place," Cal said.

"Where's Ben?"

Cal looked immediately at Riley, who cringed.

"He's on assignment."

"Yeah, I got that. What I don't get is why the two of you are trying not to tell me what that assignment is exactly."

Cal and Riley exchanged another glance. "How was the first day of treatment? You look—"

"I didn't go."

"What?"

"Answer my question."

"I just came to see how you were doing, and bring some dinner, I—"

"Where. Is. Ben?"

"We... He... There was some discussion about what's happened — happening — to you. We thought we might be able to get some answers from someone with a little more... someone who knows a lot about Station. Its history."

Van slumped into a seat on the couch. "Who knows more about Station than you?"

"Van—"

"Just tell me."

"My predecessor. And what do you mean you didn't start treatment?"

He shook his head. Never a complete answer. "Why do you think she knows something that you wouldn't? You've been at Station for like 10 years now."

"She was there for 30."

Van looked back and forth between the two of them. Despite everything he'd told them, they still held out hope. It was hope borne from ignorance, but, it was still hope. Van tried to remember when he'd lost that kind of faith. Somewhere around his first week in residency, he was sure.

"So where is she, your predecessor? Where is she now?"

It was storming in Washington, D.C. Ben wasn't used to rain or the lighting and he didn't even have an umbrella. After a few passes around the block, he parked his car in a spot as close as he could find to the Tenleytown Psychiatric Hospital, a long term care facility for adults whose minds had gone far away. He shut off the car and made a dash for the front door. Security was expecting his arrival, even at the late hour, and buzzed him right in. After he passed through three different sets of locked doors, an orderly in green scrubs and tattered zip-up sweatshirt greeted him.

"You're here to see Juliet?"

"If that's Juliet Wright, then yeah."

The orderly nodded, and they started down the hall. "She's the only Juliet we have. Been here longer than me, and I've been here a long time."

"Can I ask why she's in here?"

"Juliet? She's crazy. A paranoid schizophrenic. Doesn't trust anyone. Breaks with reality, has delusions, hallucinations. She's built this elaborate fantasy world where she's a retired government agent who protected some kind of alien ship in the ocean out in California. That's where she's from."

"I see," Ben said. "That is crazy."

They made their way through a maze of corridors and more sets of locked doors before taking an elevator to the fourth floor. After another run of corridors and another locked door, they ended up outside cell number 465. The orderly peered through a tiny square window in the door, then turned back to Ben.

"She's not dangerous," he said. "Sweet old gal actually."

Ben nodded. The orderly knocked on the door and then unlocked it. He announced Ben, motioned for him to enter, and then shut and locked the door after him.

The room wasn't what Ben expected. There was a bed in the corner, a couch along one wall and some book shelves next to very sturdy looking desk. A television sat on a small stand across from the couch. If it weren't for the cinder block walls covered an inch thick with foam green paint, he would've even called it homey. A white-haired woman in a pair of Tenleytown standard issue pajamas sat at the desk, working under the faint light of a lamp with a stained-glass shade. She didn't turn around.

"Ms. Wright? I'm Ben—"

"I'll be right with you. Have a seat please."

Ben took a seat on the couch. Wright scribbled something in a note pad at her desk. In front of her, on the wall, she'd tacked up dozens of sheets of paper, each covered edge-to-edge with numbers and equations and graphs. Ben couldn't make out the details from his seat, but he reasoned he probably wouldn't understand them anyway. After a few more moments, Wright spun around in her chair.

"What can I do for you?"

Ben introduced himself and, in case the orderly could over-hear their conversation, kept up his cover as a detective at the Metro Police Department.

"I don't think so," she said.

"I'm sorry?

"You're from Station One." Ben glanced at the door, but Juliet continued: "He can't hear us."

"How do you know I'm from Station?"

"I can smell it. How is everything holding up there?"

"Things have been better."

"Yes, I heard of the tsunami. That was the singularity's doing?" Ben nodded. "We always feared it something like that. And the dragon?" Ben nodded again. "Things were never that exciting in my day. The most we ever had to deal with were the occasional class twos getting loose and causing a bit of panic. You boys certainly seem to have your hands full."

Ben looked for something to say, but Juliet wasn't quite what he'd expected when Cal told him where she'd been living. He detected a bit of an accent, but very faint and he couldn't place it. Her features were, though well-worn with age, exquisite: high cheek bones, startling green eyes, a slender frame. In another life Ben could've imagined her as a model or an actress.

"If you don't mind my saying so, Ms. Wright, you seem…"

"Not crazy?"

"For starters."

"Call me Juliet. Crazy is a relative term. I assure you, I am quite nuts. Just not in the way the good doctors and nurses here at Tenleytown assume."

"Good to know."

"So, you have a grand purpose for this dramatic late night visit?"

"One of my colleagues, he's very sick. There's reason to believe that the singularity or maybe the ship have something to do with it. But we've searched Station's medical records and not found any other cases like his."

"Your friend, he's dying?"

"He's pretty certain of that, yes."

"And what makes you think Station has anything to do with it?"

Ben explained about the scans and the size of Van's tumor and how impossibly quick it had grown. Juliet listened carefully, but seemed unimpressed.

"We've spent our lives, you and I, dealing with the fantastic. It clouds our perspective, makes us look for the extraordinary in perfectly ordinary things," she said. "Sometimes people just get sick."

"So, you don't remember anyone at Station with a strange illness, then?"

"Now I didn't say anything like that. We are talking about Station One. I saw plenty of things that if pressed to save my life by explaining them, I probably couldn't."

"Well Van—"

"Van? Jacobs? Van as in short for Evan, Evan Jacobs, the doctor?"

Ben eyed her very carefully. The look on her face at the sound of Van's name unsettled him. It was a mix of horror and concern and delight, the look of a fox who'd been dropped into a henhouse. He took a soft approach. "You know Van?"

"Can you get me out of here? I'm suddenly in the mood to visit San Diego."

Cal was even more resistant than Riley to the idea of Van foregoing treatment. After an hour of arguing, he eventually agreed that, in the end, it was Van's decision to make. The three of them sat silently in Van's living room afterward, waiting to hear from Ben. It was nearly 1 a.m. when Van excused himself to his bedroom.

He stripped off his T-shirt and tossed it on the floor. He was hot, sweaty and his stomach had been doing flip-flops ever since he smelled the food Cal had brought. He had a half-dozen pill bottles on the counter in his bathroom, and he scanned them quickly for the one that would help tame his nausea. He found the right bottle, downed a few of the pills and, when he lowered his head, saw Cal, in the mirror, standing behind him. He jumped a foot in the air.

"We should put bells on you," Van said.

Cal indicated the pill bottles on the counter. "You okay?"

Van turned to face him. "I wish you wouldn't have done that."

"I did knock—"

"No, I mean Ben. I wish you wouldn't have sent him off on some goose chase."

"Why do you think its a goose chase?"

"I don't want to go through this with you again, Cal."

"Do you want to die?"

"What kind of question is that?"

"You didn't answer it."

"What I want is irrelevant." He brushed past Cal and back into his bedroom. "Hope and faith are not treatment plans."

"I know this is… there are things you don't yet understand, things—"

"That's the problem. All the secrets. I mean… is your name even Cal? I know nothing about you."

"So, you're upset and I do what? Throw years of protocol out the window?"

"Don't try to make this about me."

"It's always been about you."

"I don't think you can even tell what the truth is anymore. Putting aside everything you don't tell me, how many times have you lied to me?"

"I'm just trying to do what's right, for everyone," Cal said.

"Yeah, you've got an odd way—"

Before he could finish, the building quivered, and then it shifted violently, knocking them from their feet. Van grabbed the side of his bed and pulled himself upright. Out the window, the sky was bending.

"Sir, I really don't think I can do this."

Ben had spent the last five minutes, speaking as fast and using as many large words as he could, explaining why the night orderly needed to allow him to leave Tenleytown Hospital with Juliet Wright.

"Do you see this?" Ben said, waiving a couple pieces of folded paper in the orderly's face. "It's a writ of *habeas corpus* that demands I produce the patient in pursuant to Chapter 41 Title 22 Section 33 Annotated Code of the District of Columbia in Superior Court immediately for a hearing on her right to collateral estoppel."

"Collateral... what? It's after midnight."

"Ever hear of night court?"

He reached for the papers. "Can I—"

"Man! I do not have time for this. Do you want to call the judge and tell him why, when the bailiff calls his hearing to order in exactly 22 minutes, his witness, the only witness, isn't there to take the stand? Do you?"

"No, but— Sir, nobody told me anything about a transfer. They said you were coming to talk—"

"I'm telling you, now. Do you want to speak to the judge? Here." Ben made a show of pulling out his phone and dialing. Then he thrust it at the bewildered orderly. "Here ... you do know what *res judicata* means, don't you?" The orderly shook his head. "*Habeas corpus*? No? Then how the hell are you going to talk to the judge?" Ben put the phone up to his ear. "Yes your honor... I know Your Honor..." he cupped the receiver and turned toward the orderly. "What was your name again?"

"You know, just let me call my supervisor and I'm sure we can straighten this out."

"Oh, fine. We'll do this your way." Ben punched him in the face, and he fell to the ground, unconscious.

Juliet stood, staring.

"I tried to do it the easy way," Ben said.

"Indeed, indeed."

"You ready?" She nodded.

Outside in the car, Ben asked if she thought Van was going to be okay. Juliet thought for a moment. "I don't think he's got to worry about cancer."

Van lay on his shower door. Everything hurt, and he didn't want to move. He had the all-too-familiar taste of blood in his mouth, and what was usually a steady tick-tock of time in his head instead bobbled like a buoy on the water. The sensation bewildered him. He had to grasp something solid, he had to ground himself. It had been just a few seconds, hadn't it?

The break had folded space and pulled the building with it, that much was clear, even to Van. It had fallen, tipped — probably just the top half judging from the angle they were at — and he'd tumbled from the bedroom all the way through the bathroom door. He heard Cal moaning, but he couldn't see him.

Carefully, he shifted his weight so he could pull himself up. He strained to reach the towel rack on the wall and prayed it would hold him. He latched on, pulled hard and swung himself off the door, just as it shattered. He hung there, in the air, muscles screaming. The building groaned. He smelled smoke, mixed with the sickeningly sweet aura of cinnamon.

"Give me your hand," Cal said.

He was on the side of the bathroom doorframe, reaching down. Van took his hand, and Call pulled him through the door and into the bedroom. They lay on the wall, breathing hard. Cal scrolled through some readings on his comm.

"Six or seven breaks in the area," he said. "They dissipated fast."

"Foreshocks."

"What?"

"I think we're leaning on the building across the street. Where's Riley?"

"She was still in the living room."

Van called out to her, but she didn't respond. The building shifted and dropped, bouncing them into the air. Van didn't know how far they'd fallen, but it was far enough. They had to get out. Once everything settled again, he clambered his way down the piles of shattered furniture toward the bedroom door.

With Cal's help he boosted himself through and grabbed the doorframe. Slowly, they climbed together through the hallway, using cracks in the drywall and broken floorboards as hand holds and steps. It took a few minutes, but eventually they reached the living room. It was as a bad as he'd imagined: Riley lay prone on top of the windows along the west wall, separated from a drop hundreds of feet to the ground by an inch of cracking glass.

10

Riley stirred. Her eyes flickered open.

"We're coming, Riley, we're coming!" Van shouted.

"Yes, thank you. I'd much like to be going now," she said.

Cal grabbed him by the arm, holding him back. "How are you going to get down there?"

"Carefully. And preferably without one of us dying."

They climbed through the kitchen and onto the back of the refrigerator, which had fallen and lay against the upside of the center island. It shifted under their weight and Van realized that if anything — a floor plank, a light bulb — fell loose and hit the windows, they'd shatter.

"Maybe I should go alone," he said. At least that way, they'd lessen the chance of sending something hurtling toward Riley. Cal nodded, and Van pulled himself to the edge of the counter so he could survey the situation. Riley lay not far from one of the cement support columns along the window-wall. It was more than twenty feet away, but it looked intact. If he could jump to it…

"No," Cal said. "I know what you're thinking. No."

"I don't see any other way."

"If you miss, you'll kill her and yourself."

"I won't miss."

Van stood, teetering on the edge of a two-inch thick slab of granite counter top. He looked back at Cal, and then jumped. He hit the column feet first, but his legs slid in opposite directions and he fell forward, smacking his face and groin on the cement.

The fall stunned him. Slowly, he turned his head to the side, watching as the cracks in the glass spidered farther around Riley. He reached his arm out to hers, but he couldn't grasp her hand. She shimmied closer, millimeter by millimeter, and he leaned out over the glass as far as he could while still keeping a firm grip on the column. Their hands clasped just as the glass shattered. Riley swung like a pendulum through the window frame, dangling from Van's arm, her weight separating his shoulder in the process.

He screamed, but gathered himself enough to yell at Riley to not let go. Just as he felt he was about to black out, Cal leaned over him and grabbed her by the arms. He pulled her onto the column and Van rolled onto his back, cradling his arm.

Van looked up at Cal. "Good thing one of us can land on his feet."

The three of them sat on the column, staring at the ground below. Van asked Cal to help him pop his shoulder back in place. Than, carefully, he tried to rotate it. The pain made him grimace.

"Can you climb?" Cal asked.

Van nodded. He didn't have a choice.

They scaled the broken furniture and debris in Van's penthouse until they made it to the hallway and back up into the bedroom. From there, Cal used his body weight to turn a large crack in the wall into a hole big enough that they could all pass through and out into the hallway. They'd planned to take the stairwell as far down through the building as possible, but water flowed from broken pipes like a river, blocking their path. Instead, they went up the two flights to the roof, then down to where the edge of Van's building had punched through into the one it was leaning on. They ended up on a deserted office floor. There was no power, so the elevators weren't working. It took an hour to descend the fifty flights of stairs to the ground level.

Outside, Van hardly recognized his neighborhood, though he was sure at least part of his couch lay in the middle of the road. While his building had toppled, others were just gone. Riley stood in the middle of the street, trying to gather data on what had happened.

"I'm having trouble keeping my comm link, I think we're caught in a phase distortion wake."

"What the hell does that mean?" Van asked. "Is it still happening?"

"I can't tell. But it means we leave, now."

They walked the eleven blocks to Station One in silence. The streets were hollow and empty; the few people they passed on the way were either dead or running, from what and to where, Van had no idea. When they finally arrived, Riley was set to start parsing data, but Van insisted she come to sickbay first.

She sat quietly on the edge of exam bed while Van sutured her arm, a gash she'd gotten when the window broke. He'd already put a few butterfly bandages on another cut on her forehead.

"Sorry 'bout your arm," she said.

Van shrugged. "I've dislocated it more times than I count. Old surfing injury."

"Does it hurt?"

"Yes. But I'll be okay."

"You almost died."

"I think that tends to happen when you're in a falling building."

"No, I mean, trying to save me. When the break hit, I tried to run for the hallway. But my leg buckled and I fell. A pot hit me in the head and the next thing I knew, I was lying on your windows."

"It's not your fault."

Van finished placing the last stitch in her arm, and then he wrapped it in a roll of gauze.

"We've got to stop this."

"We will."

"No, we won't."

"Riley—"

"Your treatment—"

"I don't have anything to test it on, remember?"

"Yes you do. Me."

"What?"

"You've tested earlier permutations on humans."

"On brain-dead trauma victims. There's no way—"

"We need to know if it works. If we don't at least try, it won't matter what happens to me anyway, will it?"

"I have no idea what it'll do to you."

"I almost got you and Cal killed tonight, all because my leg doesn't work. Before that I got you buried under a desert. Even if we somehow survive all this, I'm not sure I could go on knowing that I'm putting everyone around me at risk."

"There's no guarantee it'll work. And then, it could take days, weeks, before you see any signs of improvement. We'll be gone by then."

"Do you want to die, having not even tried?"

She was resolved. He could tell by the look on her face. He pulled off his latex gloves and went to the cold storage locker. He'd made three vials of the new serum Walter had designed, back when he still had hope that he'd get to test it on the neural fibers that made up the containment unit.

"I cloned the stem cells myself. Spared no expense."

She smiled. "From what?"

"My cheek."

He asked her to lie back, and then he cut a slit in her jeans, exposing the scar the road sign had left in her thigh. He started an IV line, and then, loaded a syringe with the serum. He attached an EKG to her chest, put a blood pressure cuff around her arm and an oxygen monitor on her ring finger.

"You sure?" he asked.

Riley nodded, and Van injected the drug into her IV.

"How long will it take?"

Van checked the level in the saline bag. "I want it all to run through, so about ten minutes. But you're staying here for the foreseeable future, so I can monitor your vitals. We'll have to take some blood in about 24 hours to run some tests, too. Just, don't tell Cal about this, okay? Until we know if it worked. And certainly don't tell Mark A. Cooper."

"Mark A. Cooper?"

"He's the attorney for the family suing me for doing exactly this to their son, the one Zora said is missing?"

"That's a coincidence."

"What do you mean?"

"Mark Cooper was one of Cal's old aliases, back when he spent more time in the field."

Van left Riley and made a straight line for his office, but Carlos intercepted him on the catwalk. How'd he been? Was he feeling okay? Had he heard from Ben? He was on a top-secret mission somewhere, probably Europe, you know?

"Carlos, why are you here so late?"

"Riley says a senior staffer has to be here monitoring the field grid in the water. It was my turn for the night shift. I was here when the breaks hit."

"Where's Cal?"

"I haven't seen him since you all came back. Is Riley all right? You look okay."

"Give me a heads up if you see him, okay?"

Carlos nodded and Van left him standing alone on the catwalk. He shut himself in his office, took a deep breath and then called out to Walter. As usual, the computer greeted him.

"Transfer command functions of the Station One mainframe to my control," Van said.

"This is a priority one action that requires medical override authorization, Dr. Jacobs. Do you concur?"

"I concur, do it."

"Command functions transferred."

"Open the squad leaders' logs. Show me any references to my name in Cal's journals."

"The search has returned no results, Dr. Jacobs."

Nothing? Cal kept a super-secret journal and never once mentioned Van? He actually felt a pang to his ego. Not a few hours earlier, Cal told him that everything had been about him and now... this? Van shook his head. More subterfuge, more manipulation. He asked Walter to search for *Coram Deo*, but nothing much came up. Just a few notations every couple of months that the group remained "in hiding" and that its composition was "mysterious." Cal had made the same notes as his predecessors in his own logs, so he obviously knew about the group long before he and Riley had rifled through Kyle Owens' war chest.

"Walter, search for references to Mark A. Cooper."

The name turned up in Cal's journals a couple hundred times, but the only hit in the last year — a document attached to a log file — came just about three months ago, a day before Cal showed up in Van's emergency room on a gurney. Van asked Walter to open it, and the lawsuit that had been filed against Van popped up. Had Cal really orchestrated everything? Was that how his patient's family knew he'd treated their son with an unapproved drug? Cal had told them?

He was about to restore command control when he noticed a reference to "viewing the posts" in one of Cal's earliest journal entries, from nearly ten years ago. He had Walter search the logs for the same phrase and found similar entries in every Station squad leader's logs going back sixty years.

"Walter, search the library archives for postmortem examinations."

"Search returns code dark, do you wish to unlock and decrypt, Dr. Jacobs?"

"What the hell's code dark?"

"Code dark is a classification of secret compartmentalized information that returns nil to all users who lack command control, it was established in 1921 by—"

"Thank you. Unlock and decrypt."

A series of medical charts and autopsy photos spread across his screen. The patient was identified only by the number 12. Van scrolled through the photos. They were black and white, grainy, and cracked. He couldn't make out much. Why classify this stuff so no one but the squad leaders would even know it existed? The last photo was the inside of some guy's chest cavity. Van almost moved right passed it, to the autopsy dictations, when an odd detail caught his eye. He looked close at the guy's heart. Or hearts, rather — he had two of them and they were both in the wrong place.

Van fell back into his chair, jaw dropped. This wasn't a human's autopsy.

Van burst into Carlos' office.

"Walter, open a schematic of Station One," Van said.

A map appeared on Carlos' screen. He looked up at Van like he'd lost his mind. Probably not real far from the truth. He walked around to Carlos' side of the desk and pointed to a blank section below the garage levels, at the bottom of the schematic. "What is this?" he asked.

"Uhm, the schematic you asked for?"

"Carlos!"

He looked close at where Van was pointing. "Nothing, it's rock. Ground."

"Then why do the surrounding corridors cut off, like they're leading somewhere. Why build hallways to nowhere?"

"Dude, is this like a personality change from the tumor or—"

"Do we have any older plans, from the 40s, 50s?"

"You're looking at the official one, right here. We didn't implement version control of our files until a few years ago, so if it was different back then, the changes are probably lost."

"Maybe they were lost intentionally."

"What's going on?"

"Walter, are their any schematics of Station One classified code dark?"

"What the hell's code dark?"

"There are fifty-four schematic diagrams of Station One classified as code dark, Dr. Jacobs. Do you wish to unlock and decrypt?"

"Fifty-four?" Carlos asked.

Van turned and left. He took the elevator as far as it would let him go and when it stopped at the bottom, he instructed Walter to let it drop farther. As he did when Van transferred command control, Walter warned that descending to Station's dark levels wasn't something one did on a whim. He asked for Van's confirmation, then released the lift to sink down into the depths underneath the building.

When the elevator opened, the corridor in front of him looked like all the others inside Station: dark, narrow, artificially lit. At the far end, it opened into a vestibule with a garage-sized door on the opposite wall. When Van reached it, it rose automatically. He stepped inside.

The room was vacuous. The air, chilled and stale. He called for the lights, and spots on the walls faded in around him, flooding the edges of the room. Then, one-by-one, twelve individual circles in the floor began to glow, each illuminating a water-filled tube and a naked, alien body. Van's knees wobbled.

"Now you know all my secrets," Cal said, from behind him. Van turned, slowly. "So it's come to this? Mutiny? Return my command control."

His face was austere, his lips pulled tight. Van knew the look, Cal was livid. Made sense. He took a step back into the room, putting some distance between the two of them.

"Van, you heard me, give me back the computers."

Evil. Wrong. Execrable. Appalling. So many words came to Van's mind, but they all meant the same thing. "All your secrets? I don't think I'm even close."

Cal stepped into the room, and Van took another step back.

"I'm not one of the bad guys, I know you don't believe that, but—"

"Why do they look like us?" Van turned back toward the

twelve tubes, all lined in a giant circle in the center of the room. The aliens were tall and hairless, but that's where the major differences ended. They had olive-colored skin, two arms and two legs, pairs of big, round eyes, noses and mouths. Van's hands trembled.

"Van, command control, now."

"Answer my question!"

Cal clenched his jaw and tightened his fists. Van braced himself for a fight. The last time he'd tussled with Cal, it'd been a toss-up. At least that's the way he liked to think of it. That was better than admitting a man fifteen years his senior had come very close to kicking his ass. But then, Cal softened.

"We share a high amount of DNA," he said.

"We... share... we share DNA?"

Cal nodded.

"How is that possible? How much DNA?"

"A lot."

"What are you saying?"

Cal didn't answer. Van took a few unsteady steps away from the aliens, away from Cal. The room was spinning, he was sure. Or he was falling. Neither was a good. The next thing Van knew, Cal had stepped up and put his arms on his shoulders, steadying him.

"Van, the computers. Restore my command control. I'm not going to ask again."

Up front and direct Cal was a lot scarier than sneaky, secretive Cal. Van was in no mood for a fight. He told Walter to restore command control, then asked how Cal knew where he was.

"Walter's transfer protocols require he notify me when I've been demoted in the command hierarchy. Unlike some of my staff, he always does what he's told."

"I'm sorry, I just…" He glanced over at the aliens. "What happened to them?"

"The first team to make its way inside the ship found their bodies. They'd huddled together in a stasis chamber just under the bridge, probably some time after the crash when it was clear they weren't flying that thing out from under the ocean."

"They were dead?"

"The stasis chamber was functioning when the first team boarded but we were never able to wake them up. Over the years they just quietly died, one by one, the last in 1948."

Van took a few tepid steps toward the tubes. The one directly in front of them had a Y-shaped incision in its chest, so that was the one whose pictures he'd seen. Number 12.

"You kept this from us…"

"For good reason."

"What gives you the right?"

"I have every right!"

"Sure," Van said. "The greater good. But Ben, Riley, me? You can't trust us?"

"Obviously not."

"I trusted you… Mark. You've been manipulating me from beginning."

Cal's eyes grew wide. His mouth dropped open. "I had to make sure you'd agree to help us."

"You could've asked!"

"I don't leave things to chance. I'm glad you trusted me Van. And somehow, I'm going to prove that your trust wasn't misplaced."

"You owe me more than that."

"I don't owe you anything."

Cal barked some orders to Walter, shutting down the lights. He told Van to follow, and Van did, without argument. They walked the length of the corridor in silence and took the elevator back to the operations deck. When they stepped out, three men holding semi-automatic weapons and wearing black tactical gear stood, waiting. Van looked over at Cal.

"So this is how it's going to be?"

Cal didn't look at him. "Take Dr. Jacobs to the brig," he said.

If there was a bright side, it was that Kyle Owens was snoring in his cell when the tactical team hauled Van in. He was locked away less than an hour when Riley, cane in hand, came down the steps, looking like someone had killed her puppy.

"What is going on?"

"What are you doing out of sickbay?"

"Looking for you! What is happening?"

"Please try not to wake up sleeping beauty over there, that's all I need."

"Cal's lost his head. I've never seen him like this."

"Are you all right, feeling okay?"

"I feel fine. What is going on?"

"Cal's angry."

Riley shook her head. "I think, I think he's hurt. His feelings, I mean."

Van scoffed. "I doubt—"

"Just, tell me what's happening. Why'd he put you in here?"

"Because I deserved it."

"No, I don't buy that for a moment. How long does he plan to keep this up?"

"You'll have to ask him, Riley."

"Why won't you talk to me?"

He looked around at his new accommodations: the steel bench along the wall, the grey walls, the hovering dots of electromagnetic energy holding him captive. He stood and walked toward the edge of his cell, to face Riley eye-to-eye.

"I took control of the mainframe."

She almost laughed out loud. "You did not. Oh, I can't imagine that confrontation."

"He was really calm about it, actually. Eerily calm. Almost like he'd anticipated it." Huh. Maybe he had. Van wouldn't put it past him.

"What did you find out?"

Van shook his head. He wasn't prepared to reveal answers to the universe's mysteries to anyone, even Riley. "I found out… that we're… like some kind of dysfunctional family," Van said. It was a true statement, at least.

"Yeah, especially when two of the brothers are shagging." Van's eyes grew wide. He stammered. "I'm codding ya," she said.

"Really?"

"No, absolutely not."

"How did you know—"

"You just told me."

He was tired. Normally he would've seen that coming. "I…

we… shots. There were lots and lots of shots."

She smiled. "Right, and I'm next in line for the throne of England…"

"Riley—"

"Besides, who among us hasn't had Ben, I mean the boy is—"

"Riley!"

"This time I am codding ya," she said.

"Just so we're clear, that means joking, right?"

She stepped close, and raised her hand to the edge of the magnetic field. Van brought his up, to meet hers. Riley smiled again, then turned and headed for the stairs.

"Where are you going?"

"To talk with Cal. You two boys are going to kiss and make up." She stopped. "Just don't enjoy it too much, okay?"

"Riley."

She put her hand in the air to say "as if" and disappeared up the stairs. A smile grew wide across Van's face.

"Well wasn't that a touching little scene," Kyle said from across the room, still laid out on his bench, eyes closed. Van rolled his eyes, then took to his own bench and settled in.

Cal had sat at his desk, doing nothing in particular, for more than an hour. His jaw hadn't loosened since he'd ordered Van into the brig, he couldn't concentrate on work and now, Riley was yelling at him. He caught enough of her tirade to know she was upset about Van and thought very little of him for the moment, but man, she could talk fast when she got going.

"Are you finished?" Cal asked, after she finally came up for air.

"You can't do this."

"This doesn't concern you."

"Since when?"

"Did he tell you what he did?"

"I found it a bit amusing, actually."

"I'm glad treason strikes you as funny."

"Come on, Cal, let's compare. Was it any worse than the things you've done?" Riley folded her arms across her chest and pursed her lips. Totally silent, for once. Cal glanced at the clock on his desk; it was almost five in the morning. The sun would be up soon.

"What are you talking about?"

"I don't know *Mark*, what am I talking about?"

The silence was sharp. Riley stood in front of him, arms still crossed, glaring.

"Have you manipulated me the way you have Van? Ben? What's the truth here? Do you even know anymore?"

Cal didn't get a chance to answer, because sirens sounded on the operations deck. Riley dropped her arms to her side, took a last look at Cal, then left. He followed her down the stairs and they both quickly scanned through the warnings and alarms on Walter's screens.

"Massive cascade failures in the EM field grid, delta section. It's collapsed," Riley said.

"Delta, that's the section that—"

"Faces the coast."

11

Van woke suddenly, still in his cell. He never could sleep well sitting up. Kyle, though, was missing. His cell was empty.

"He's fine," Cal said, coming down the stairs.

"What did you do to him?"

"I wanted to make sure we had some privacy."

Van rolled his eyes, sat back down on his bench and stared up at the ceiling. "Okay, well, what do you want?"

"I had my reasons, you know."

"So did I."

"Fair enough. But your reasons were idle curiosity and a rebellious streak that, admittedly, I failed to crush. Mine were altruism and the preservation of humankind."

"Altruism? You keep your secrets for you."

"You don't know anything about me."

"That's what I've been saying."

"Like or not, most people — most governments — aren't ready to accept the idea that we didn't come from some god sitting in heaven."

"You don't have the right to make that choice for everyone."

"Then who does, you? This is beyond the two of us," Cal said. "I'm doing the best I can."

"You think it would destroy us. Maybe it would unite us. You don't know."

"You're right. I don't."

That wasn't the answer Van had expected. Cal hit the locking button beside Van's cell, and the force field blinked off.

"This isn't by choice. Ben's still in the air and Riley needs to be here, saving our collective asses. So that leaves you. I need you."

"What's happening?"

"The world is ending."

Ben watched Wright doze on and off in her seat, waking herself up only when her snoring got too loud. They were in a private plane of course, a small charter Station One kept for the rare times they had to travel any great distance. Ben was about to turn back to his magazine when the copilot came back to the cabin.

"There's some kind of disturbance in San Diego, the airport has shut down. We're being diverted to LAX."

"No. We can't do that. It'll take hours to drive from Los

Angeles to San Diego."

The pilot shook his head. "There's not really an option here. The airport is closed."

"Can I use your radio?"

Ben followed the pilot to the cockpit, and he adjusted the controls on their radio to an emergency frequency that Station monitored — but no one answered when he tried to raise them. He reactivated his comm and tried to connect to Station's computers, but he couldn't. He couldn't even locate Van or Cal or Riley, for that matter. He turned back to the pilots.

"How long until we're on the ground?"

The police shut down Park Avenue, the street that runs alongside Balboa Park from Hillcrest to downtown San Diego, on both ends. Emergency vehicles littered the road near University Avenue, and a small crowd — a few nuts who weren't smart enough to have already fled — lined the police blockades, trying to get a closer look. Van was impressed the city had mustered any response at all, considering the last weeks. The police waved Cal and Van through the tape line.

"It's nighttime in there," Van said as they stood on the crest of the canyon, where the park dipped down into the valley. A cloud of darkness hung in the air, casting a fog of shadows over everything. What had been a neatly manicured lawn was now an overgrown forest choking on vines and ground cover. Van couldn't totally see what was happening beyond the tree line, but the air churned violently and lightning blasted the sky, every few seconds.

"I can't get a lock on the edges of the break," Van said, looking at the readings on his comm. "The temporal disruptions are too big, but I think it's — it's actually growing."

As they tried to get a grasp on the situation, a burly white-haired man in a black fireman's uniform stalked toward them. He said he was the chief, and he demanded they tell him what was happening.

"A noreaster," Cal said. "A localized severe weather system that's… settled in the park."

"We're in the Southwest."

"Would you believe El Niño?" Van asked.

Before he could answer, a roar erupted from somewhere in the park, shaking the ground. Even Cal flinched at the sound.

"What the hell was that?" the chief asked.

"That sounded bigger than a dragon," Van said. He looked at the chief. "You should move your perimeter back."

"How far back?"

Another roar burst form the park. It was closer this time.

"I hear the Palm Desert's nice. Hot this time of year. But nice."

The ground rumbled in pulses. Then, the trees directly in front of them toppled as the head of a large animal with scales and fangs and two flaring nostrils popped out. It paused for a moment, turning its head to the side long enough to get a good look at them. No one moved. Then, it roared. The chief and the crowds behind them scattered. Van and Cal stood their ground.

"Is that a dinosaur?" Van asked.

"Looks like it."

"I miss the dragon."

It bellowed again, shaking the nearby buildings all the way through to their foundations.

"I thought San Diego was under water when dinosaurs lived on land?"

"It doesn't necessarily work that way."

The dinosaur stepped toward them abruptly, pinning them against one of the abandoned fire trucks. Then, it turned on its hind legs and stomped down the road, disappearing into Hillcrest.

"What do we do?"

"I don't know."

"Cal?"

"Let me think!"

He started pacing in a little spot on the road. He stopped only long enough to answer his cell. "Yeah, yeah, put her through . . . . Madam President. . ."

Cal shot him a look and rolled his eyes. Van leaned up against the trucks to wait. Unless she planned on flying out here and wrestling the dinosaur and probably, more likely, dinosaurs, to the ground, she was just wasting the last bit of time they had left.

At Station, Riley tried to hold it all together.

Van was on the phone, and he sounded scared. She had nothing but bad news to deliver. "We're seeing multiple breaks all over the region. They're not dissipating," she told him.

"Cal's still on with the president. I can't tell, but I think the break here is expanding. We're falling back. You've got a solution on the horizon, right? Riley?"

She wanted to lie to him.

"We're out of solutions. No more stopgaps."

The words left a bad taste in her mouth. An alarm went off on one of the monitoring stations across the room. "Van, I gotta go. Keep me updated, okay?"

She hung up and took a look at the screen. The last section of the field grid, the one facing north east, toward Los Angeles, was about to fail. There was nothing she could do.

"Walter, has Ben's flight landed yet?"

"No, Riley. Estimated time of arrival is in twenty-three minutes."

"Do they have enough fuel to turn back to another airport? Las Vegas?"

"No, Riley."

Behind her, on the office level up above the operations deck, someone moving caught her eye. She looked up. It was that Asian girl who worked in the lab, wasn't it? What was her name… Anna? Surely she knew that no one was up there. Riley was about to call out to her, but a break erupted in Tijuana, diverting her attention. Then another, and another. The whole Baja peninsula was about to be swallowed.

After just a few seconds, she forgot all about Anna.

Van leaned against the truck, listening to Cal try to calm the president. He was on the line for a good ten minutes before finally hanging up and breathing out a long sigh. He looked over at Van. "She's declaring martial law, sending in the military."

"What good will that do?"

"Would you like to call her back and argue the point?"

Hardly. He pulled his sunglasses off and rubbed his eyes, trying to massage the pain out of his head. Maybe it was that he hadn't slept much and it'd been a few hours since he'd eaten, or that he was keenly aware that he was dying, or that the world was about to end before that happened anyway, but he was starting to feel a little woozy. He focused on the seconds in his head, trying to keep them straight and ticking steady, lest he pass out. He waited for Cal to pace into a plan and start barking orders.

That's when the sky exploded behind them. Van found himself on the ground. He rolled his head to the right, where Cal lay unconscious. He sat up, slowly. Behind him, the cloud of darkness that had enveloped Balboa Park was swirling and rising toward the hole burning in the sky. Riley would probably have some term to describe it — two separate breaks merging under their own gravitational forces. Van had no term for it, other than bad. He crawled to Cal and did a quick head-to-toe check. No blood, no obviously broken bones. Van tried to rouse him, and after an disconcertingly long time, he came to.

"Tell me that wasn't what I think it was," he said.

Van shook his head, and then helped Cal to his feet. Just thirty yards away, charred and smoking, was most of a very large, white H, leaning against the side of a building. Down the road, Van spotted a D and parts of what, he assumed had been the

two Os from the Hollywood sign. That didn't bode well for Los
Angeles. Cal didn't notice the letter though, he was distracted by
the sky. It was half darkness, half fire, filled by two breaks twisting and surging toward a collision.

The smoke billowed over Riley in viscous waves, stinging her
eyes and choking her lungs. She was looking at the ceiling, she
thought. She was definitely on the ground. Why was it so quiet?
Her ears rang. She felt heat. Something was on fire. She pushed
herself up and struggled to get some bearing. Over there, across
the room, was where that girl stood. Anna. Riley shook her head.
People around her were screaming, she just couldn't hear them.
Anna had blown up in front of them. The smoke was suffocat-
ing. She wobbled to her feet and staggered over to a control
panel. She called for Walter, but couldn't hear if he'd answered.
She looked around. The fire suppression system wasn't working. This wasn't a break, it couldn't have been. The smoke was so
thick. Someone flailed his arms at her, screaming, begging for
help. His voice was soft, distant. Riley tried to move, but her legs
wouldn't do as they were told. She fell to her knees, grabbing for
the remains of the nearest workstation to hold herself up. Then,
she heard a clicking sound high above her, then a clunk. Her
hearing was coming back. People were screaming. The clicking-
clunking sound kept repeating, over and over again. She looked
up, toward the office level. Anna. That bitch had tried to blow
them up. She couldn't think of a worse time for a bombing.

Bright beams of light bounced around the ceiling, and then the floor around her. Flashlights. People were coming in. She heard the clicking again, but this time instead of the clunk, she heard a whirl and then a low hum. The wind whipped up around her and the smoke swirled toward the ventilation system high in the ceiling.

The flashlight beams grew brighter as a half-dozen people poured into the room. She heard a voice call out to be careful, that the support structures weren't stable. No shit. She tried to focus on them. They all had guns — but not just guns, hunting rifles. Not a rescue team. She fumbled around for the pistol she had strapped to her back, but a voice interrupted her: "I'd like to see your hands, my dear."

She was blinded by the man's light, but she didn't need to see his face. No one could mistake the syrupy sound of the Reverend Sinclair's voice.

Van and Cal couldn't reach Station One.

"I'm sure everything's okay, I'm sure—" Van's cell phone rang. He checked the caller ID and saw that it was Riley. The voice on the other side of the phone, though, sent a chill down his back. Van tensed, as did Cal when he saw the look on Van's face.

"Where's Riley?"

"She's here," Sinclair said, "she's fine, which is much better than I can say for the rest of your band of heretics."

"Let me talk to her."

"Oh Van. You do have one-track mind. Here." He heard a shuffle on the other end of the line, then Riley's voice.

"There's a half-dozen of them, all armed. They bombed—" There was struggle, then Sinclair was back.

"She's a feisty one."

"You've accomplished nothing, Reverend."

"Really? Because from where we're standing, we're in the thick of it all."

"Whatever you did, you put the mainframe into lock down. You won't be able to access any systems."

"The systems we want aren't here."

"Then what do you want?"

"I want for you and I to take a little trip together. Just the two of us."

"Why would I do that?"

"Because you've got a lot of people over here still alive and I suppose you'd want to keep them that way."

Sinclair gave Van a few instructions, which he relayed to Cal after hanging up. He was to meet the Reverend at the Airport in Little Italy, alone. Cal refused.

"Do you see a choice here?"

"The choice is that we don't negotiate with this guy."

"He'll kill them. He'll kill Riley."

"He's going to kill them anyway."

"If I go with him, if we separate him from his people, it'll give you a chance to take back Station."

"What's left of it."

Van looked up at the sky and the two breaks creeping toward each other. "We can't put the universe back together until we're back in control."

Cal pursed his lips. "Go," he said, finally. "And Van?"

Van shook his head. He didn't want to hear it. "Go, help Riley," he said.

Except for a few police cruisers, Van didn't see many other cars on the streets as he drove to the airport. It was the middle of the day, but the tear in the sky had blocked most of the sun. The storefronts in Little Italy were empty, though all the lights were still on, and some doors were even propped open. Some people stood on their balconies and watched, but they were the exception, the few that had dared venture outside out of the very few who'd stayed behind.

As he crested the hill, he saw the airport and the remains of what he guessed was probably a 747. There were no emergency trucks, though, no ambulances or police cars. Just the smoking corpse of a jet liner lying on the runway.

He parked the car in the cell phone waiting lot and walked the last quarter-mile to the terminal. It was mostly abandoned. Security was non-existent.

The escalators down to baggage claim weren't moving, so Van decided to save some time and walk up them to the second level, where the gates were. He turned left at the top, and walked the length of the empty corridor, all the way to the end where it opened into a large, half-circle shaped room. Sinclair was alone, standing and smiling at the far end, in front of gate 41.

Van headed toward him, but got only part way before a group of people surrounded him, pointing rifles and shotguns. Van recognized a few of them from the days he spent locked in the basement of Sinclair's church. He put his hands in the air, but kept his eyes locked on the Reverend. They patted him down and removed both guns he kept under his blazer, plus the backup pistol strapped to his ankle. Satisfied he was defenseless, they marched him the rest of the way across the terminal.

"Good day, Van," Sinclair said.

"Fuck you."

"Language. There's no need to be hostile."

"The first chance I get, I'm going to kill you. A lot."

The Reverend bellowed. "I knew we were on to something when we found you. I had no idea it would be something so special."

"Could you just shoot me now?"

Sinclair's smile vanished. "Can't you show me the least little bit of respect? I am your elder."

"Could you just shoot me now, *sir*?"

"No, Van. I cannot. I've got a job for you, first. Let's go."

They led him down the jetway and out onto the tarmac, where a helicopter sat waiting. Van stopped dead.

"You're not serious. Flying? That's suicide."

"We are pressed for time. There isn't another option."

"How about just not flying, you lunatic."

"Get on the chopper, Van."

He looked back at the six guns pointed his way. They were going to kill him, either now or later, but later meant Cal and Riley had that much more time.

"Where are we going?"

"There's a little alien ship out there on the bottom of the ocean, and I'd like to see it if you don't mind. I trust you know the way?"

"What do you want with the ship?"

Sinclair's face grew long. It dawned on Van, for the first time, that the man was in his sixties. He didn't look it most days, but for just that one short moment, the weight of his life flashed in his eyes.

"Because I need to destroy it, Van. It just has to go."

12

San Diego grew small in the distance as Van and Sinclair flew out across the ocean. The pilot, one of Sinclair's men, stayed low in the sky, but the chopper still bounced and shuddered, buffeted by the breaks.

Van sat in the back, his hands cuffed. Sinclair sat in the seat opposite him with a .22 nestled in his lap and a backpack at his side. After about 40 minutes, they reached the dry dock. When they landed, Sinclair strapped on the pack, uncuffed Van and then pointed the gun at him.

"Let's go," he said.

"No."

"No? Maybe you missed the gun?"

"Shoot me. Whatever. But you can't get on that ship without me, so the threat seems idle."

"Well I guess we've found ourselves at a bit of an impasse."

Van crossed his arms. He had no doubt Sinclair would eventually shoot him, but dead or alive, the only way he was getting to the ship was to dive into the water and swim down there.

"Good thing I took out a little insurance policy, then." He pulled his phone from his pocket and showed it to Van. "I'm to make a phone call in two hours from the time we left the airport. When I make that phone call, I will tell my associates to disarm the explosives we planted in what's left of your headquarters. Believe me when I say it's enough C4 to blow a hole in the side of a mountain. And I will make that call, Van. Assuming you've taken me down to the ship and I've returned, safely. Or, we can just sit here and see what happens." He looked at his watch. "We've got a little over an hour left."

Van visualized kicking him in the balls, then taking his gun and hitting him with it until he made the call. Sinclair was stubborn, though, he'd probably sooner let Van beat him to death than give in. He pulled out his comm and accessed the controls for the airlock, the one that contained the lift. Sinclair made a point of showing Van that he was leaving his cell phone on the seat in the helicopter.

"Shall we go?" he said, a creepy smile plastered across his face. A moment later, the two of them were on the lift alone, drifting downward.

"It won't work," Van said.

"What's that?"

"Destroying the ship. You'll just make things worse."

"The gates of hell have opened. You think things could get much worse?"

"You have no idea."

He grinned. So confident, so arrogant.

"I'm only doing the Lord's work," he said.

"Sure. He tell you to kill a bunch of people, too?"

Sinclair jumped from his seat and grabbed Van by the collar. "I wouldn't expect a heretic like you to understand!" As suddenly as he'd surged, he calmed, let Van go and settled back into his seat. He took a moment to straighten his tie. "Death is an unfortunate, but necessary part of war, Van."

"So now you're fighting a war?"

"There are always wars to be fought. Demons to exorcise."

"You're a lunatic."

"And you play with forces meant for God alone. I don't think we're all that different."

Ben had never been to the Metropolis, it was a backup center—more like an emergency bunker—built in the Hollywood Hills, near the reservoir, years before his time. It was meant for a situation just like this one, a calamity. He wasn't sure when anyone had even been there last. Their pilots had diverted to Burbank Airport when the tower at LAX failed to respond, and then he and Juliet spent a good amount of time convincing a local news crew to do a good deed and fly them across the city in their helicopter.

He found the electrical panel, and pumped the primer handle to get a charge and power the computer systems. When he finished, Walter greeted him and asked if he wished to activate the Metropolis' command functions.

"Yes, and start locating all of our people."

"Please identify," Walter said.

"It's Ben."

"I think he means me," Juliet said.

"Walter, this is Juliet Wright, she—"

"Ben, please confirm the presence of Juliet Wright."

"Why?"

"Confirmation required in ten seconds, please confirm."

"Or what?"

"Do you know what's going on here?" Juliet asked.

"He's never done this before. Yes, Walter. I told you this is Juliet. Why?"

"Confirmation received, thank you."

A steel grating fell across the main door, the only door. An alarm sounded, and all of Walter's primary control screens locked down.

"Walter, what are you doing?"

"Executing security protocol 9-3-Golf-1."

"Which is?"

"Termination of Juliet Wright."

The half-dozen goons Sinclair had left behind at Station One had released Kyle from the brig. They bound Riley's arms and he stood over her, a shotgun propped against his shoulder, while she sat cross-legged on the floor. He was on his cell phone, giving Katie the rundown on how the plan had gone.

Some plan it was. They'd brought down a large part of the second level in the blast, cutting off the elevator. The primary control screen was scattered across the deck, just chunks of glass now, but part of the secondary control still worked. The central power conduit must've been damaged, because the emergency power indicators were flashing. Walter was down, though every once in a while, when Kyle wasn't grinning at her, she stole a glance at his system profiler. Her vision was a bit blurry, and the profiler was a small part of the secondary control, which was across the room, but it looked to her like Walter was regenerating. Theoretically, more than half of Walter's memory and process cores could be obliterated and he'd still be able to repair himself. She didn't know, though, how long it'd actually take. The progress bars, and there were dozens of them, were still near their bottoms and one was flashing red, which meant it probably required intervention on her part.

She also didn't know where they'd taken the rest of the staff. By her count, three on the operations deck had survived. There were maybe another four or five scattered throughout the other levels, but most of Station's team wouldn't be able to offer much if any resistance, especially against a group of shotgun-wielding fanatics. There were too many to hold in the brig, and with the power fluctuating, the force fields wouldn't hold anyway. Maybe the labs or the holding bays... The holding bays. The force fields. The color probably drained from her face, because Kyle looked at her funny.

"Something wrong, Little Miss?"

She shook her head. Not yet.

The lift met the airlock on the outside of the ship. After the pressures equalized, Van opened the doors. They had less than forty-five minutes for Sinclair to get back to the surface and make that phone call. They'd never make it.

"I think you know where I want to go," Sinclair said.

The whole trip was probably more than a mile considering the way the passages twisted and turned around themselves. Van admonished the old man to pick up the pace more than once, even as he knew they were close, just because he could. When they arrived outside the singularity chamber, Sinclair was winded and quiet. Van opened the doors and he and Sinclair stepped inside.

The room was nothing like before. The air was unsettled, hot. The walls of the containment unit rocked as though something pounded its insides. Every few seconds, the room shook. When Sinclair saw the containment unit, he swallowed hard. His hands trembled.

"Everything you expected?"

"You know, part of me didn't believe it was real. Even when we stepped through the airlock and I was standing on an alien ship, I didn't believe it." He turned to Van, who'd been standing beside him. "I want to see it."

Van activated one of the sphere's control panels and shut down the white cloak in the containment unit's walls. The color dissolved and the singularity came into full view. Van almost gasped. It was ferocious and spasmodic, easily more horrible than the last time he'd seen it — and he hadn't really cared much for it then.

"It's quite beautiful," Sinclair said.

Van turned to him. "So now what?"

He opened the shoulder bag he'd been carrying and showed Van the contents: several small, grey slabs of metal.

"What are those?"

"The antimatter devices you all have kept locked away in your labs for the last decade."

"Please tell me you're not this stupid."

"Do you believe in God, Van?"

His eyes were locked on the singularity. Van thought carefully about his answer. "I did."

Sinclair glanced briefly his way, then nodded, as though Van's answer made all the sense in the world.

"You can't do this. This isn't the way. You have to let me—"

"Yeah," is all Sinclair said. Then, he spun on his heels and cracked Van across the forehead with his gun. Van collapsed to the floor, spitting blood. The worst part was that he hadn't even seen it coming.

Sinclair loomed over him, a fat blur of rage wielding a pistol. "At one point, I'd had high hopes for you," he said. "Too bad things aren't going to work out."

Van railed against the pain in his head, heaved his leg up and cracked it against the side of Sinclair's kneecap, toppling him and sending the gun spinning across the floor. Van scrambled to his feet, but he was woozy. He staggered just a few feet before falling again. The last thing he saw before blacking out was Sinclair, standing over him, gun back in hand.

"Walter, stop. Disengage," Ben said. The ventilation fans, somewhere in the ceiling, clicked off. Walter was shutting down life support. He was trying to suffocate them.

"I'm sorry Ben, I am unable to comply."

"Are we sealed in here?" Juliet asked.

"It's air tight. Walter, disengage and restore life support."

"I'm sorry Ben, I am unable to comply."

Ben slammed his hands down on the primary control. Nothing he did would unlock the screen. "Walter, shut down. Immediately!"

The air already felt thin. Each breath was harder than the last. Juliet took to the door, but the steel grating had latched to something deep in the concrete floor.

"Walter, I gave you an order."

"I'm sorry Ben—"

"Disengage all security protocols!"

"The security protocols cannot be disengaged."

Ben felt light-headed. Juliet slunk to the floor, her breathing labored, as the air in the room evaporated. "Can you cut the power?" she asked.

"That won't bring life support back."

"What systems do you have access to?"

"Nothing primary. Anything major is locked."

"What about minor?"

Ben glanced across the room. The secondary controls were still online, but he couldn't do anything with them. "Ah, core utilities programs, the library archives, the system profiler, that's it. Nothing with any command function."

"The system profiler?"

Ben nodded. "Why?"

"It has a safe mode, does it not? To disengage malfunctioning units from the rest of the mainframe? It's low priority and might not be blocked by the security protocol."

"I'm not following you."

She was nearly breathless. "If you unseat the life support systems from the mainframe, trick it into thinking they're malfunctioning, you should be able to reset them manually."

Ben crawled his way across the floor to the secondary control. His vision was blurry and dark. He ran his fingers over the controls, trying hard to concentrate and hit the right buttons. Juliet was right, the safety mode of the system profiler hadn't been locked by the security protocol. He put the life support systems in maintenance mode, and then unseated them from Walter's control. Now they just had to restart the system.

"By the electrical panels," he said, gasping. "There's a primer handle in the box labeled ECLSS, flip it."

He watched as Juliet crawled, painfully slowly, to the electrical panels. She pulled herself to her feet and grabbed what he hoped was the right handle. She flipped it down, then back up before collapsing on the floor. The fans in the air vents clicked back on, and Ben felt the air start to move again.

He took a few moments to catch his breath, then asked Walter who had implemented security protocol 9-3-Golf-1.

"9-3-Golf-1 was implemented by the Director, Ben."

"Cal."

"That is correct."

No one but Riley heard the first roar, it was too soft. The second and the third, though — they all heard those. Kyle's face turned ashen grey. He looked down at Riley, sitting quietly on the floor.

"What was that?"

"Our dragon."

"Your dragon?"

"Mmm-hmm. We've been keeping it sedated in a holding bay on the 40th floor. I imagine, though, that when your bomb blew our main power conduit, the drug diffusers in the bay's life support systems went down, too. It's probably awake now. And very grouchy."

"You can stop it."

"With what, exactly? You don't know what it took to get it here."

"So, what do we do?"

"I'm going to sit here and watch what happens. If I were you and you were intelligent, I'd probably run. But we both know what's wrong with that notion, right?"

She winked at him. Kyle gulped.

"Listen here—"

The wall behind him, the one with the corridor that led back to the labs and down to the sub-levels, burst as the dragon's head barreled through. It took out two of Sinclair's men in single spray of fiery breath, then knocked Kyle across the operations deck with its tail. He landed in the water filtration system. The three remaining goons scrambled for the stairs, but the dragon dispatched them as it did the first two.

Riley pushed up to her feet and backed against the far control panel, her hands still tied. The dragon turned an eye toward her, then stalked down the stairs and across the platform. Its snout came within inches of her face. She trembled, fighting the urge to scream.

The dragon sniffed her, once, twice, then once more. She started singing, an old Irish lullaby her mum had taught her, just as she had all those times in the holding bay. It snarled and showed its teeth. Riley flinched and her voice cracked at the sight, but she kept singing, hoping it would recognize her voice. Then, slowly it backed away, crossed the room to the pile of debris it had left scattered as it burst through the wall and — after turning in a circle three times — curled up in a ball and closed its eyes.

Riley kneeled to retrieve her cane from the floor, then took a few tentative steps across the room. The dragon opened one of its eyes and glared, only to close it again and go back to sleep. She glanced around to find Kyle, then rummaged through his pockets until she found the keys to the shackles they'd put her in. After a bit of wrist-bending gymnastics, she managed to unlock them and free herself.

She glanced back across the room. The dragon was snoring, but that didn't mean it wouldn't wake at the slightest provocation. She took a deep breath, and then crossed to the secondary control panel. One of Walter's processing cores had fried when the main power conduit blew. She disabled it and tried to bring the backup cores online, but no luck. They just wouldn't engage. She slammed her hands against the panel.

"You break it, you buy it."

The voice startled her; it was Cal with a group of armed men in military fatigues. They'd climbed up the elevator shaft and were standing in the rubble, guns raised. Big guns. Riley went to Cal and wrapped her arms around him "You're okay. Where's Van?"

"With Sinclair. Giving us the chance to rescue you, but it looks like you don't need rescuing." He looked over her shoulder, across the room. "Would that be the dragon, asleep on the floor?"

Riley stepped back. "Yeah."

"Okay, then."

"Walter's down and the main processing core is totally out. I can't bring on the secondary systems for some reason and his regeneration routines have stalled."

The smells of scorched flesh and pulverized rock wafted about, a nauseating, ever-present reminder of what she'd just been through. Her knees wobbled as the adrenaline drained away. Cal reached out to steady her, but she brushed him off. She was going to stand on her own, no matter what it took. Cal scanned the few functioning display screens and consoles. "Ben's landed in LA so we transfer command functions to him at the Metropolis substation." He set to work at the only fully functioning computer panel in the room and after a few moments, had Ben on screen.

"What happened there?" he asked.

"Suicide bomber," Riley said.

"Ben, I'm going to transfer Station's command funct— Who the hell is that?" Cal asked.

On the screen, Juliet stepped up behind Ben. "Hello Calvin, glad you're not dead. Are you surprised we're not?"

"You brought her with you?!"

Ben looked at Juliet, then back at Cal. "What's the problem?"

"The problem is your mission was to extract information, not extract her."

"It's good to see you, too, Calvin."

"Ben, are you okay? Did—"

"Yes, we're *both* okay. Where's Van?"

"With Sinclair," Riley said.

"Charles Sinclair?" Juliet asked.

Ben turned to her. "You know who Charles Sinclair is?"

"Calvin hasn't told you?"

Three sets of glaring eyeballs landed on Cal. "Juliet, shut up."

"Tell us what?" Riley asked.

"Charles and Calvin go way back, to his time at the U.N."

"That's not true, is it?" Riley asked.

Cal sighed. He looked at Riley. "I met Sinclair in Rwanda, before I came to Station One. He was a missionary there."

"Why hadn't you said anything?"

"Sinclair had been in hiding for a long time, I was hoping I wouldn't have to."

Juliet scoffed. Cal glared at her. Riley folded her arms and turned away.

"Cal, where did they take him?" Ben asked. "Where is Van?"

When Van opened his eyes, the gun was still aimed his way. Sinclair pulled the trigger, it fired, the bullet burst from the chamber but then, everything slowed. The singularity flashed, and the room broke apart. Van wasn't on the ground anymore, but standing next to Sinclair, looking at the containment unit. He was talking: "It's quite beautiful," Sinclair said.

Van looked over at the Reverend. In a second, he was going to hit him with the butt of his gun. Van decided, instead, to hit him first. He cracked him with his elebow, and Sinclair stumbled but still managed to turn and aim the pistol. Van grabbed him at the wrist and forced the gun into the air. He rotated his body in, keeping the weapon safely pointed at the ceiling, and then cracked Sinclair in the face. The old man tumbled, and Van had the gun.

"Fool me once," Van said.

"You kill me, your friends will die. They'll never disarm the bombs unless I tell them to."

Van fired, three times. Sinclair collapsed, his eyes frozen, open as big as moons, as though Van shooting him had been a true surprise. Van watched as he took his last breath.

"Maybe they won't have to," Van said.

Before he could decide on his next step, his comm buzzed in his pocket. He hit a few buttons, and Cal and Riley appeared on his screen, Riley looking worse for the wear and Station in ruins behind them.

"Where's Sinclair?" Cal asked.

"Dead. Are you back in control?"

"We've secured Station, but we're crippled. Ben's at the Metropolis in LA, we're routing comm signals through there for now."

"They laced the place with explosives. You've got minutes, maybe less."

Silence, then finally: "I understand. Can you regroup with

us in LA? Are you okay?"

"I'm fine. How's Riley? Can she hear me?"

"Van!" Riley said. " I can hear you. Tell me you're all right."

"He didn't hurt me. At least, not in this timeline."

"How fast can you get back to land?" Cal asked. "Riley thinks she can realign the parts of the field grid that haven't burnt out from LA."

Van looked back at the singularity, its pulsating waves of light and energy crashing against the walls of the containment unit. "I don't think we have that kind of time," Van said.

"What's happening down there?"

"Hey, Riley, that bomb theory. It would need to be placed on the event horizon, someone would have to get close, right?"

"No," Cal said.

"The containment unit's going to fail, Cal. You're not going to make it to Los Angeles. You're not going to make out of San Diego, no one is."

"Nobody who's ever entered the containment unit has survived," Riley said.

"I understand that."

"Van, I am ordering you not to do this."

"It's for the greater good, right?"

"Van—"

"Guys. We don't have any other options. Time up."

"Yes we do," Cal said. "We have options. Get your ass out of that room and off that ship."

"It's okay. Really. It makes sense that it's me, that I'm the one."

"But—" Riley said, nearly in tears. "Ben is here with someone who might be able to help you…"

"It won't matter much if this thing tears the world apart. You know I'm right, Cal," Van said. "You have to get out of there."

The singularity flashed behind him, and this time the entire ship rocked. Another flash hit and Van was almost thrown from his feet. He steadied himself. "It'll be okay. I'm okay."

Cal seethed. For a moment, he looked like he was about to yell more orders, but then his features softened, and he broke his gaze. He looked over at Riley, then at the screen and toward Van. He nodded.

"Could you tell Ben something for me? Tell him I don't know if the answer was yes, but it wasn't no, either. He'll know what I'm talking about."

Riley nodded and Van said goodbye. He ended the transmission and then started gathering the explosives Sinclair had stolen. He activated the controls in front of the singularity and started the procedure — at least, he hoped — to open a door in the containment unit. It took some trial and error, but eventually he got the sequence right. Its clear, round walls turned solid red and from somewhere, a deafening alarm blared.

Van pushed the control panel out of his way and took a small step forward. The singularity thrashed so violently it sounded like a locomotive. He took a deep breath and steeled himself to move closer, just as a hole spun open and sucked him inside.

Time flowed. Palpable, textured. It swooshed around him, smooth like a rabbit's fur at once and grainy like sand paper the next. Van stood in a calm field with electric-green grass and a startling blue sky. The singularity hovered in front of him, a black mass that twisted the air and sucked long streams of black smoke from a great distance. It seemed both in front of him and behind him; above and below. It was far away, and close. Nothing moved, yet everything did.

And he wasn't alone.

One of the aliens stood watching him, its arms comfortably at its sides. It was bigger than Van, taller, but so familiar. They shared genes, a common point of ancestry. They were the same. All Van could think to say was "Hello." It didn't answer. "Can you understand me?" Van asked.

"We understand you," it said.

"You speak our language?"

"You speak our language," it said.

"I'm speaking English."

"And what is English? A derivative of the Origin."

"The Origin? What's the Origin?"

"We are the Origin," it said.

The singularity burst forward, and the boundaries of the space shifted around them. Van saw reflections of his past; he saw himself walking toward the singularity and entering the containment chamber at the same time. Then, as quickly as it had happened, calm settled back over them. Everything had changed, though. The size of the field, the movement of the air, Van's position relative to the singularity. The alien was either unaware or unphased, because it continued talking:

"We are the beginning of you, of your species in time and space. Our language was built into the genetic code we planted on your planet millions of years ago. And like you evolved, so has it."

"You created us."

It nodded.

"Why?"

The alien cocked its head to the side, curiously, as if it were taking notice of Van for the first time, looking him up and down.

"Why not?"

The singularity burst again, and the landscape shifted violently around them. Van steadied himself, not completely sure which way was up and which way was down. They weren't in a field anymore, but on cold glacier, surrounded by water and under a purple sky. The black hole was the only constant.

"Your ship, this singularity. They're destroying our planet."

"A solar flare from your sun disrupted our navigational equipment and we skimmed the Earth's gravitational field. The spatial harmony inside the chamber was disrupted, the singularity shifted and the containment unit was damaged. We crashed."

"Are you trapped in here?"

"We are not here. There is no 'here.' Space, time are both moving and stopped, both broken and whole."

"So, you're... not trapped in here?"

"I intended to fix the breach, but I have failed. The damage is too severe."

"How long ago?"

"There is no 'long,' there is no—"

"Yeah, yeah. Look, you made this thing, can't you shut it

down?"

"It is an extraordinary point, a rupture in spacetime."

"Well… un-rupture it."

"We designed the singularity to exist."

"What's the alternative? Let it keep growing until it eats the entire universe?"

The alien cocked its head to the side again. "Good point."

Van dropped Sinclair's bag to the ground, kneeled down and pulled out the pieces of the antimatter bomb. It was made of three, amazingly heavy slate-grey squares that when stacked together, formed a cube. He twisted the final piece into place and a blue LED display showing just ten seconds clicked on, shining through the cube's skin. Just ten seconds. Seeing the numbers made everything that more real. When he looked up, the alien was standing next to him.

"You would sacrifice yourself?"

"It's nothing that heroic. I'm dying," he said. "I have cancer. A mass in my brain."

"You have a gift."

Van looked up. "I'm sorry, a what?"

Cal and Riley hurried to gather a few essentials from the storage lockers before they evacuated. Riley kept one eye on Cal, then, finally stopped and turned to him. "I think it's time you level with me," she said. "You know more about what's happening with Van than you've let on."

"No, Juliet Wright does. That's why I sent Ben to talk to her."

"And Sinclair?"

Cal sighed. "We thought, once upon a time, that there were things about the ship, about the aliens, that the world needed to know. We felt if we recruited religious leaders like Sinclair, they could help us, help everyone better adapt. They could be our ambassadors. It was a psyops move."

"And how'd that work out?"

"Most we approached didn't take it well. Sinclair really didn't take it well. Before we realized what we'd done, a mostly harmless zealot had turned into a time bomb."

"So you burned him?"

Cal nodded. "We did everything we could to discredit him professionally, publicly and eventually, I think he realized what he was fighting against and he just went away. I'd thought for good. I let my guard down and then he showed up and shot me."

"The very night you set out to recruit Van. Quite a coincidence."

"Van's not like you and me. He's an anchor. That's why he can tell when breaks shift time around him."

"I don't understand."

"One of Juliet's crowning achievements at Station One, aside from weapons of mass destruction, was a genetics experiment code named Fusion. For all intents and purposes, she created Van."

"What do you mean, she created him?"

"Through *in vitro* fertilization, with genetically modified gametes."

"Modified with what?"

"Alien DNA."

The alien stood calmly as Van's mind filled with questions. A gift? The constant of time in his head? He wasn't dying?

"You grasp time unlike any of your race. You are evolving."

"Evolving? I'm not dying?" he asked.

The alien leaned forward and touched him on the forehead. Van didn't understand how, but he knew, in that moment, it was telling him the truth. The biopsy on the tumor had been inconclusive and the genetic markers didn't match, but at the time he'd chalked it all up to a lab error or sloppy work. If the mass were something different entirely, though, if it weren't a cancer at all…

"I'm not dying."

The alien shook its head. "Do you still wish to sacrifice yourself?"

"What?"

"We can allow you to leave."

"You can get out? Why are you still in here?"

"There is no 'here,' there—"

"Okay, all right. Whatever." He looked over at the singularity. It roiled in the air, so much power for something so small. Time really was up, and he had to see this through. He twisted the top slice of the bomb a full 180 degrees, intending to start the countdown, but the clock stood at 10 seconds. He looked up at the alien.

It sighed. "Still, you cling to your human perceptions of time."

Van rolled his eyes. If it had to be the hard way, it had to be the hard way. He reset the clock to zero, then started toward the singularity. He stopped at the last moment and glanced back at the alien. It nodded, giving its approval.

Then, Van took a final step forward.

The singularity pulled him apart. He saw the edges of the universe and the folded strings that formed the basis of reality. Light ceased to move; it floated around him as if he were swimming in it, as if he could hold it. He wasn't scared.

He was calm.

He felt no worry.

He just was.

But it had to end. He squeezed his hand around the detonator and the bomb tore through his hand, then his torso, then his head.

Blackness.

THREE DAYS LATER

Cal watched from the windows of the lift as it lowered deep into the ocean. They'd made it to Los Angeles to meet up with Ben and Juliet, but then had been trapped there after the president declared martial law in San Diego and most of Southern California. Not long after they'd lost contact with Van, the breaks that had opened around the region simply faded away, but the damage had been done. Most of the city was still standing, Cal noticed, as they were escorted through the empty streets. But large portions were simply missing: half a skyscraper, there, entire neighborhoods here. It looked like the aftermath of an earthquake, except something had swooped in and taken the debris away.

Cal's comm showed the ship had no power, so they couldn't open the airlock doors when the lift attached. They'd come prepared for that, though, and used a laser torch to cut through the outer hull. It took more than an hour. Life support wasn't functioning either, so Cal made it clear they had to be in and out as quickly as possible or they'd risk running out of oxygen.

Flashlights in hand, he, Juliet, Ben and Riley — walking without a cane — began the journey in the dark toward the singularity chamber. When they made it, they found the containment unit still standing, but lifeless, a giant glass ball guarding over nothing.

"Over there!" Riley shouted. Her flashlight had settled on a body, but it wasn't Van's. "Is that—?"

"It's one of the aliens," Cal said. "One of the ones from this ship."

"Why do they look so, so… human?" Ben asked.

Cal didn't answer. He looked at Juliet. She returned a grim smile. He flashed his light about the room and they came across more bodies, all of them dead. He counted no less than six. One of them was Charles Sinclair.

"Who are these people?" Riley asked.

"My guess? They're all the ones who've entered the chamber since the ship crashed here."

"But, there are no signs of decay. Some of them would've

been in there for decades."

"I know," Cal said.

Ben busied himself shining his light into all the corners of the room. Then he checked and double-checked all the bodies they'd found. "Van's not here," he said. He turned to Cal. "Where is he? Cal?"

Cal didn't answer.

"Cal, where is Van? If he went inside there, where is his body?" Ben asked.

Cal shook his head. "I don't know."

"Is he…? How do we find him?" Riley asked.

Cal shook his head. "We don't."

He turned and headed for the door, leaving Riley and Ben in the wake of his pronouncement. Juliet followed him into the outer corridor.

"What are you going to do?" she asked.

"I don't know."

"This wasn't his path."

"Of course it was. He took it, didn't he?"

"Do you believe in destiny Cal?"

Destiny? He'd seen time bend and break and fold over on itself so many times, the idea of a fixed point at the end of it all seemed… ridiculous. He thought about it for a moment.

"For Van's sake, I will now."

It wasn't much. But it was something.

JUSTIN McLACHLAN

Journalist. Writer. Superhero. Okay, maybe not that last one. My days can be lonely. It's usually just me, the dogs, *King of the Hill* on Netflix and my keyboard. To make things interesting, I take frequent walks down the street to the convenience store just off the 15 freeway, because, well they're the only people I know.

To them, I'm "that guy who writes." Occasionally, I'm also "that guy who comes in seven times a day to buy diet Dr Pepper and protein bars," or "that guy who really likes diet Mountain Dew" and sometimes "that white devil who refuses to pay cash for anything."

I prefer the first.

But, it makes me wonder, how does anyone know that I'm a writer? How do I know I'm a writer? Sure, I have that t-shirt that says as much, but truthfully, the guys at Steve and Barry's will sell those to anyone.

There's this book, my shorts stories, and all the stuff I do for magazines, papers and Web sites like Wired, Popular Science, Sharelseuth.com, San Diego Citybeat, voiceofsandiego.org, etc. That's probably good proof, too.

Oh, and I'd love to hear from you. Find me on Twitter, I'm @justinmclachlan, or Facebook at facebook.com/thatguywhowrites. I also spend time at justinmclachlan.com.

SHORT STORIES FROM
JUSTIN McLACHLAN
Thought Patterns
Next Year
Sitting for the Superkids

AND FROM
BOXFIRE PRESS

Kuro Crow, by Dave Maass
Curtains, by Shauna O'Connor
Sic Transit Gravitas, by L.G. Fitzgerald
A Fear of Flying, by J. Allen Scott

CPSIA information can be obtained at www.ICGtesting.com
Printed in the USA
BVOW021136130912

300374BV00002B/1/P